DATE DUE

BATTLE BORN

ELEMENTALS:

BATTLE BORN

BY

AMIE KAUFMAN

HARPER

An Imprint of HarperCollinsPublishers

Elementals: Battle Born

Copyright © 2020 by HarperCollins Publishers

Illustrations by Levente Szabo

Library of Congress Control Number: 2020933730
ISBN 978-0-06-245804-9

Typography by Joe Merkel
20 21 22 23 24   PC/LSCH   10 9 8 7 6 5 4 3 2 1
❖
First Edition

For Kate

Who's been listening to my stories almost as long
as I've been telling them.

CHAPTER ONE

✳

COMING TO CLOUDHAVEN HAD BEEN A GOOD IDEA. Anders and his friends were sitting together just inside the entrance hall of the dragons' ancient stronghold, wolves and dragons all in human form. Somehow, impossibly, they were safe—at least for now.

None of them had spoken much since the Battle of Holbard. They'd just trekked out of town, rested for as short a time as possible, and then flown here to hide, dragons exhausted and wolves shaken. Most of Holbard had been destroyed today, the city left in ruins by the clash of the Snowstone and the Sun Scepter. There had been injuries on all sides.

Everyone was hurt, and everyone was afraid, and Anders knew the only way out was to convince all his friends to work together—to stop the fighting once and for all. He also knew that the longer he let the silence draw out, the harder it would be to break it.

"So . . ." When his voice interrupted the quiet, the others blinked and looked up.

Anders had hoped he would know what to say once he had their attention, but now they were all staring at him, and the words came no more easily.

"We need to figure out what to do next," he said awkwardly.

"We need to get all the way inside Cloudhaven," Ellukka said immediately, leaning forward. "We're not safe out here in the entrance hall, we're too exposed. I don't know how they'd get up here, but the wolves will be hunting us. They think we attacked the city."

"You *did* attack the city," Viktoria pointed out stiffly. "We all saw you fly in with that . . . that *thing*. It put huge cracks in the ground—there was *lava*!"

"That was the Sun Scepter," Rayna shot back immediately. "And we needed it because the wolves were using the Snowstone to cool all of Vallen and attack the dragons. Your Snowstone caused at *least* as much damage with its ice."

"Speaking of dragons," said Theo, "the Dragonmeet might think the same as the wolves—that we were trying to attack the city. But when we don't come back to Drekhelm, they're going to come looking for us. They're not going to be happy once they realize we're not on their side."

"Then whose side *are* you on?" Sakarias asked quickly. "Are you with the wolves?"

"We're not on anyone's side," Anders said, raising his voice a little to be heard over the wave of muttering going around the circle. "Or I mean, we're on *everyone's* side. We don't want to help the wolves *or* the dragons attack each other. And we have to stick together. We only have each other now."

Seven wolves sat on one side of the circle, four dragons on the other. Plus Kess the black cat, of course, who was currently in Rayna's lap, batting at the ends of her hair with one playful paw. Of all of them, only Kess seemed to have no worries.

It was night, and their faces were dimly lit by the row of runes that circled the big room just below the domed stone ceiling. The runes were carved into the rock itself, and they glowed a gentle turquoise.

Anders ran his gaze around the group, letting it rest on each of them for a moment in turn.

Rayna was leaning against her friend Ellukka, her head resting on the bigger blond girl's broad shoulder. Ellukka had months of experience flying, but Rayna had only transformed for the first time a few weeks before, and she was exhausted by the distance she'd covered today, and all the days before as they'd hunted for the pieces of the Sun Scepter.

Anders saw Ellukka swallow hard. The last they had seen of her father, Valerius, he had been badly injured. The Drekleid, Leif, had been helping him struggle back toward Drekhelm. There was no way of knowing if they'd made it.

Along the wall from the two girls sat Theo and Mikkel. Mikkel was running one hand through his copper hair, studying the wolves thoughtfully. Restless as ever, Theo was pulling open their bags as the silence drew out. He began to unpack them, taking stock of what supplies they had. The dragons had managed to grab a few things before they'd left Drekhelm. The wolves hadn't even been expecting the battle, let alone that they would have to flee from it, and they had nothing.

Next, Anders's attention shifted around to the wolves. Anders's old roommates, Viktoria and Sakarias, sat together. Det, Mateo, and Jai sat farther along, quiet and a little wary. For once, none of them had an easy joke to offer.

Only Lisabet sat by Anders's side. Just as there were fractures and mistrust between the wolves and the dragons, there were cracks separating the two of them from the rest of the wolf pack as well. Anders and Lisabet had sided with the dragons weeks earlier at Drekhelm, driving away their Ulfar classmates.

They had done it to save the lives of their friends and the lives of the dragons, but Sakarias's arm had been in a sling until just recently, and Anders wasn't sure they were forgiven. It felt like all he'd done since discovering he was an ice wolf was run and hide and fight.

"If you really want to know what we need to do next," Sakarias said suddenly, "we need to eat." A couple of the wolves snickered, breaking the tension for a moment, and Sakarias's own mouth twitched in a small, tired smile. "I know I talk about food a lot," he said, sheepish, "but this is going to be a problem really soon. It already *is* for us, if the dragons don't want to share what they have."

Mikkel sat up indignantly, fixing Sakarias with a scowl. "Of course we'll share," he snapped. And just like that, the small smiles were gone. "What do you think, we're just going to watch you starve while we keep it all to ourselves?"

Viktoria immediately came to her roomie's defense. "How are we supposed to know what you'll do?" she asked sharply. Her parents came from the wealthy west side of Holbard, and she'd always been posher than most of the other students at Ulfar Academy. Now she wielded her icy tone like a blade. "You just attacked our city. Why should we expect you to feed us?"

"I think," said Lisabet quietly, "we'd better talk about who did what at the battle just now. And why."

Together, she, Anders, and Rayna recounted what had happened over the last few weeks, while Mikkel and Theo started a fire in the big hearth. The entrance hall was a cold and miserable place to sit—it didn't even have a proper door to the outside, just an open archway that led to the dragons' big landing pad. The real shelter lay beyond a great wooden door that only Anders and Rayna could pass through. When their friends had tried earlier that day, the floor had crumbled clean out from beneath their feet.

Mikkel and Theo did their best with the fire, though, and it shed a little warmth. Someone had left wood laid out there, and flint to spark it hanging from a piece of string, as if they expected guests to come along who would need to warm themselves—though the dust everywhere told them that the guests had never shown up.

It was a complicated story that Anders, Rayna, and Lisabet had to tell, from Rayna's transformation, to Anders's and Lisabet's journey to Drekhelm, to the wolves joining the Finskól. Then they recounted their discovery that Hayn—the famous artifact designer and one of Ulfar's teachers—was Anders's and Rayna's uncle. That his dead twin brother, Felix, was their father, and Drifa the dragonsmith, accused of murdering him, was their mother.

They told the wolves how Hayn had doubted Drifa's guilt and given them her map, which had led them to the Sun Scepter.

"We needed it to counteract the Snowstone," Anders explained.

Jai and Mateo exchanged a guilty glance. They were the ones who had stolen the Snowstone during the skirmish at Drekhelm, though they hadn't known what it was at the time.

"Sigrid was using the Snowstone to cool all of Vallen," Anders continued. "She would have killed the dragons. And everyone was suffering—the wolves might like the cold, but the farmers' crops were dying, and families without enough fuel were freezing."

"So that's why we hunted down the Sun Scepter," his sister said. "It was supposed to warm the weather. We brought it to Holbard, so the two could balance each other, and everyone would be safe."

All the wolves and dragons around the fire were quiet for a moment, thinking back to the ruins of the city, where nobody had been safe.

"I guess we brought them too close together," Anders

said. "The lava from under the city and the ice above collided, and both the artifacts exploded. It wasn't some plan of the dragons' to blow up Holbard, though. If Sigrid hadn't been trying to kill them, none of it would have happened. We were just trying to solve the problem she created."

"Remind me not to bring you any of *my* problems," Sakarias murmured. But he had another small, tired smile for Anders. They had a long, long way to go, but Anders could see the wolves absorbing the story he had told, and he thought perhaps it helped them a few steps along the road to trusting the dragons.

Rayna brought them to the topic at hand, as she so often did. "Basically," she said, "Ellukka and—what's your name? Sakarias?—are both right. We all need to eat, or we won't be able to do much else. And we need to figure out how to get properly inside this place. We can't camp out in the entrance forever. It's freezing, we don't have anything to sleep on, and if the wind really picks up, it'll be miserable. It's not safe, either."

"Agreed," said Lisabet. "The dragons are forbidden from coming here—they have been as long as anyone can remember—and it's too high for the wolves. But if we can't go inside then it won't be much of a hiding place if the dragons decide to break the rules."

"Rayna and I will go look for a way for everyone to come inside," Anders volunteered.

"And we'll organize something to eat," Theo agreed. "Sakarias, you can help."

* * *

Anders and Rayna took one of the artifact lamps hanging on the wall near the hearth, and left the others behind in the entrance hall as they approached the huge door that led into Cloudhaven proper. It was set on the very far side of the hall, and the room was so large that the conversation of their friends faded behind them into silence, until Anders felt himself no bigger than the specks of dust dancing in the lamplight around them.

The door was made of dark wood and had no handle. There were rows of metal letters fixed into its surface, reflecting the light of the lamp back at the twins.

COME NO FARTHER WITHOUT . . .

~A TOKEN~

~TRUE BLOOD~

~TRUE PURPOSE~

The first time they had read these words, only hours ago, they had been baffled. But at least they'd managed to answer one question, and he and his sister moved confidently. Rayna pulled both her hairpins from her head, her black curls springing out even bigger than before. She handed one pin to Anders, and moving at the same time, with the tiny, engraved runes on the pins facing inward, the twins pressed them into the shallow indentation built into the door for them. *A token.* Anders's fingertips tingled as the essence inside the artifacts did its work, and with a soft click the door swung open to reveal a long hallway beyond it.

One by one, lamps were coming to life all along the hall, illuminating door after door, as well as a stone floor and walls lined with hundreds of long strips of metal that glowed a soft blue green with tiny, intricate runes. The whole of Cloudhaven was one giant artifact.

True blood was easy now—Anders and Rayna were descended from Drifa, and that seemed to be enough. Anders wondered if perhaps Drifa herself was descended from the dragonsmiths who had originally created this place.

Just before the twins stepped inside, Anders heard a soft skittering noise behind him, and he turned in time for Kess to leap up into his arms. He tucked her inside his shirt, and there she settled, a warm lump against his skin, purring softly.

"Well," he said, "that's a token and true blood taken care of. But what's our true purpose this time?" He knew that as soon as they asked for what they wanted, a path would light up along the ground, leading them to whatever part of Drekhelm could help them or answer their question. "Finding a way to get the others inside?"

Rayna nodded, then cleared her throat. "Cloudhaven, please show us a way to allow other people inside you."

Anders felt a flicker of hope as the lights dimmed. *Come on*, he silently urged the walls around him. *Help us protect our friends.*

Then the lights came up again, and rather than leading away, the path that appeared began at their feet, completed a circle around them, and then led straight back to where it had started, so they each stood inside a circle of light.

Anders wanted to scream.

What were they supposed to do now? How was this guiding them anywhere?

"Is it broken?" Rayna asked, stamping one foot inside her circle.

But they repeated the request and got the same result.

"So we can't get everyone inside yet," Anders concluded. "If the dragons show up, our friends will be trapped out in the entry hall with nowhere to run."

"Then we'll have to hope nobody shows up tonight,"

Rayna replied. "I guess we could ask about how to make it more comfortable for them, at least. They probably don't have a kitchen here, or if they do, I would *not* like to see inside it. The dust is so thick, there can't possibly be any food left that anyone would want to eat."

But a new idea had come to Anders, traveling through him with a quick fizz of excitement.

"No," he said. "Last time we were here, we asked about the way to find Drifa."

At the time, a path had lit up, but they'd had no chance to follow it, forced to run back and join the others. Now they had the chance to find out where their mother had been all this time.

Anders had spent all his life wishing he knew more about his parents—never even dreaming he could *meet* them—and now more than ever, his heart desperately wanted that chance. Their mother would be on his and Rayna's side, not the side of the wolves or the dragons. He could almost imagine her smile, her advice. It would be *such* a relief.

He ached for Hayn to be with them, but their uncle had been imprisoned by the wolves, and had disappeared during the Battle of Holbard. If he was out there somewhere, Anders had no idea how to find him. For now, the twins had to continue on without him.

Beside him, Rayna spoke. "Cloudhaven, please show us where Drifa is."

For a moment, nothing happened. And then all the lamps and the strips of metal in the floor dimmed, until it was almost completely dark. Again the twins waited, and this time when the glow returned, it was concentrated in one long strip of iron along the floor. Pale bluish green, it stretched down the hallway, then turned a corner.

Anders slipped a hand into his sister's and used the other to brace Kess against his chest, and together the three of them set off, following the path Cloudhaven had provided for them.

This was it.

After a lifetime as orphans, of never imagining they'd even know the names of their parents, were they about to meet one? Was Drifa really here? Was she still hiding after all this time? Why had she never come for them?

They hurried past door after door, the anticipation building inside Anders until it was almost unbearable. Deeper into Cloudhaven they went, the minutes ticking by.

Then they turned yet another corner and pulled up short—the path abruptly ended against a wall of solid rock.

The dead end was covered in row after row of text that glowed a soft blue, but Anders couldn't understand a word of it, and he knew it wasn't just because he wasn't very good at reading. These words simply didn't make sense.

He scanned the lines of letters desperately, heart thumping, looking for any kind of clue as to what he and his sister should do next. Beside him, Rayna was whispering under her breath, and he knew she was trying to read it as well.

"There!" she said suddenly, one finger coming up to point. "That says '*barda*.'"

Anders craned his neck—she was right. *Barda* was the word for *battle* in Old Vallenite, a language that had been spoken centuries ago. Anders and Rayna themselves were Anders and Rayna Bardasen, named after the battle that had orphaned them. Or at least, their rescuers had *assumed* they'd been orphaned in the last great battle—the twins had been found on the streets as toddlers, after the fighting had ended.

"Perhaps it's all in Old Vallenite," Anders said. "This place is ancient, after all. But we only know two words of it, *barda* and *rót*. Bryn taught us that one, remember, when we were solving the riddles to find the pieces of the Sun Scepter."

He thought of Bryn, their classmate at the Finskól and a brilliant languages expert—he could picture her now, pushing back her sleek black hair with one impatient hand so she could lean in to frown thoughtfully at some ancient text. Oh, how he wished she were here now.

"It could be anything," Rayna replied, gesturing helplessly at the words. "Instructions on how to get through the wall to the other side, another riddle like the ones on the map, or a really good recipe for all we know."

They tried pricking Anders's finger and pressing a little blood against the wall, remembering how this had activated Drifa's map, bringing it to life and making it obedient to their commands. The wall, however, completely ignored the blood.

They puzzled over other ideas, but eventually, Rayna sighed. "We'll have to figure it out later," she said. "We've made it all this time without her, we can last a little longer."

Anders reluctantly agreed. "We can't stay here all night, trying to guess what a wall wants." He ached to find a way through the rock, to find out what was on the other side—whether his mother was truly there—but their friends were waiting. And their friends had gone to battle and lost their homes today, for him.

He took one last look at the glowing words, then stepped back. "Cloudhaven," he said. "Our friends are camping in the entrance hall. There aren't any beds there, there's nowhere to eat."

"There's only one bathroom," Rayna added, making him smile.

"Cloudhaven, please take us to something that will help make this place easier to live in."

Just as they had the other times, the lights dimmed, then illuminated once more, a new path stretching away into the distance and around another corner. Anders and Rayna followed it, Kess perched on Anders's shoulder as they walked past long rows of doors set into the rock. There was no way to tell what was behind any of them, and Anders's curiosity tugged at him, but on he went.

The stone of the tunnel was dark, its edges rough, but although it might have felt like they were walking into somewhere forbidding, somewhere dangerous, Anders didn't find Cloudhaven threatening at all. In the strangest of ways, he felt completely at home here. Still, it was with a flush of relief that he saw that this time, the path ahead ended at a wooden door, rather than a rock wall.

He and Rayna exchanged a long glance, and then Anders pushed up the bar that was holding the door closed. The hinges were silent as it swung open, as if they'd been oiled only yesterday. But he barely noticed that. His eyes were on what was within the room they had revealed, and it was . . .

"What *is* that?" Rayna whispered.

Anders had never seen anything like it in his life. The room was large, as big as one of the shops back in Holbard, or perhaps the living room of a house, though Anders hadn't been inside many of those. It was completely full of what he could only assume was . . . machinery?

His heart sank as he took it in.

Wires stretched between the walls like a wild, tangled spiderweb. Some were strung with beads, others in motion, turning on little pulleys, carrying small buckets back and forth. Beneath them were huge cogs and wheels and gears, altogether comprising a strange machine that took up the whole of the floor. As he watched, a marble traveled along a small track set into the wall to his left, then plummeted down a long slide, dropping into a container that rested at one end of a seesaw. With the addition of the weight, the container slipped, slowly lowering itself and lifting the other side of the seesaw, which tapped another bucket in turn, setting it in motion.

Every part of the machine seemed to be connected to every other part. But why?

"Sparks and scales," Rayna muttered. "There's no way this can make living at Cloudhaven easier. I don't even know what this *is*, let alone how to use it."

"Maybe it controls the sorts of things we want?" Anders guessed. "Water, heat, that kind of thing? But if we use it wrong, who knows what we could break." He leaned against the doorframe, not daring to set foot inside the room.

His heart was thumping in his chest, and his lungs felt too small, like he couldn't get a proper breath. Everyone was depending on the twins to get them past the great door—to somewhere they could hide, to somewhere they could eat and sleep. To somewhere better than the big, cold, drafty entrance hall. And he and Rayna were stuck here looking at this tangle of cogs and wheels and wires that could take a lifetime to figure out.

He made a soft sound of frustration, and Rayna buried her face in both hands, her shoulders slumping. Anders felt like his very bones ached after the battle above Holbard, and the seemingly endless trip they'd made around Vallen before it, to gather the parts of the Sun Scepter. *Why* couldn't just one thing be easy?

It was a dejected pair of twins who closed the door to the machinery room once more and made their way back to their friends. As they approached the circle of firelight, nine faces turned hopefully toward them. But their hope dropped away at the sight of Anders's and Rayna's expressions.

Jai rose to their feet, red hair and pale skin glinting in the firelight as they walked over to offer each of the twins half a sandwich—all there was for dinner. Then, a hand on each of their shoulders, Jai steered them back to take their places around the fire.

Anders made himself comfortable, and Kess climbed down from his shoulder to take herself off on a circuit of the group, as if making sure nobody else had done anything interesting while she was away. The dark-brown bread of the half sandwich was turning stale, and the filling had gone soggy, but it still felt amazing to bite into anything at all. Anders tried to keep his bites small, so it would last longer.

As they warmed themselves, he and Rayna recounted what they had seen, and everybody else was as baffled as they were.

"One thing's for sure," Lisabet said. "We're not going to guess the answers to these questions. We need more information, and the sooner, the better. Right now, none of the adults will be expecting us to show up hunting for any, so it's the best time to go."

"Go?" Mikkel protested, almost choking on his sandwich. "Go *where*? To Drekhelm, where the dragons are waiting for us to come and fight for them? Or to Holbard, where the wolves think we attacked them?"

"Well, we have to do something," Anders said. "We can't just sit here."

"All right then, what do you suggest?" Mikkel pressed.

It was Lisabet who answered. "Both. We should try for the records at Drekhelm, and we should go to the Ulfar library." She paused. "Or whatever's left of it. We need to find anything that can tell us about how this place was built."

Theo nodded. "We have to look this up," he said. "None of us knows enough to figure it out alone, and we can't just ask someone. But Lisabet knows that library inside out, and I specialize in the records at Drekhelm. Between us, maybe we can understand enough about Cloudhaven to learn how to live here."

"Well," interjected Viktoria, as the group began to murmur about this idea, "as the only trained medic here, I'm banning anyone from trying to go anywhere tonight. We're exhausted, and it's not safe."

"I couldn't fly even if I wanted to," Ellukka admitted, and Anders, Lisabet, and all the dragons knew what she was really saying—that she was the strongest, and if *she* couldn't fly, nobody could.

But Anders wasn't sure that was the only reason Viktoria was grounding them all for the night. He saw the way she glanced at Sakarias, Det, Jai, and Mateo, and the way they looked back at her. He could see they wanted to talk. The wolves and the dragons might be stranded here together, but despite having taken the first steps, they were a long way from trusting each other.

"Let's sleep," said Rayna. "And be ready to leave at dawn."

Nobody could object to that. The wolves transformed so they could sleep in a pile by the fire—and, Anders was sure, so they could talk without the dragons understanding them.

The dragons stayed in human form, settling themselves in the small circle of firelight.

Anders stayed where he was a moment longer, hesitating. Should he transform as well and join the wolf conversation? Or should he let them talk without him? His friends might have risked their lives to protect him back in the battle, but that had been a decision made in the heat of the moment. It didn't mean he was completely forgiven, or that they completely trusted him.

Rayna was curled up beside Ellukka, but he realized Lisabet hadn't transformed either—she was busy building up the fire so it would last for the night, perhaps as an excuse to give the others some space. So with a soft sigh, he rose to walk one last circuit of the hall.

He made his way to the arch that led out onto the landing pad, to stare out through the ever-present mist and wonder what was beyond it. There was a weight on his shoulders he didn't know how to shake.

He felt responsible. Everyone here had trusted him, and now they had no food, no defenses, no allies, and they were being hunted by wolves and dragons. They had no hope, either, except to dig through the rubble of Holbard, through a disaster they had caused, or perhaps to sneak into Drekhelm in the hope of learning something about their hiding place.

He wondered if they should try somewhere other than Cloudhaven, but this was where their mother had last been, and where she still was, if he was to believe the glowing paths.

This place held so many artifacts and secrets. If anywhere had the answer to this mess, it was Cloudhaven.

Other places could hide them, but only Cloudhaven could *help* them.

They had no choice but to stay. But as he eventually fell asleep, staring at the embers of the fire, he felt more and more uncomfortable about their choice.

CHAPTER TWO

THE NEXT MORNING AT DAWN, THEY ALL ROSE with hungry bellies, and sore muscles from sleeping on the rock around the campfire. It was decided that Anders, Rayna, Lisabet, and Mikkel would go to Holbard together.

Anders and Rayna were going because they knew parts of Holbard nobody else did, and were used to acting as a team. After all, they had spent their lives growing up in every part of the city's streets, and frequently across her rooftops as well. Lisabet was going because she had a better chance than anyone else of successfully digging through the ruins of the library, and Mikkel was there in the hope they'd have extra supplies to carry home. All the wolves were worried about friends and family in Holbard, but they knew that the more of them there were, the better the odds someone would be spotted, so the rest of the pack loaded the research party up with questions and things to keep an eye out for if they could.

Ellukka and Theo were readying themselves for the attempt to sneak into Drekhelm. Ellukka had grown up among the dragons and knew its layout better than anyone, every crack and crevice of the mountain. Theo had a list of books he wanted to steal, and he knew his way around the archives best—their plan was to try to creep in and out without anybody knowing they'd been there.

Everyone was keen to get underway. A few items of clothing were swapped so Mikkel and Rayna weren't wearing any red—the traditional color of the dragons, and unusual in Holbard—and then they began their preparations in earnest.

"How do I look?" Rayna asked, smoothing down Theo's green tunic, which she had switched for her rust-colored one. After the battle of the day before, she needed to look as far from a dragon as possible.

As the four heading for Holbard readied themselves, the others were adjusting Ellukka's harness so it would fit onto Mikkel, and tying together the broken pieces of Rayna's harness—it had been badly burned by the Sun Scepter the afternoon before.

Once Anders had finished explaining to Kess that Holbard was no place for cats right now, Det quietly pulled him to one side. Det was Mositalan—he had grown up there, only coming to Vallen the year before for his transformation, and had the same dark-brown skin and musical accent as the Mositalan sailors who often came into Holbard's harbor. As well as being the most relaxed of Anders's pack, he also often thought a little differently. He hadn't grown up with stories of the evils of dragons, and that changed the way he saw them.

"Anders," he said softly, "are you *sure* you're all coming back from Holbard?"

Anders blinked at him, but kept his voice low as well. "Of course I'm sure," he said. "What do you mean?"

Det hesitated. "When you all go, it will only be wolves left here. Ellukka and Mikkel could send dragons for us, to attack. They—"

"They won't." Anders cut him off.

"Can you be sure of that?"

"Yes," Anders said firmly. "Ellukka and Theo gave up everything to help us try and stop the war. They deserve our trust."

Frustration welled up in him, though he tried to keep his voice calm. He had thought at least Det would give the dragons a chance, but it seemed their lessons at Ulfar had made that impossible.

"We're all there is to stop a battle even worse than the

one we saw yesterday," he said to his friend. "Believe me, I wish an adult were here to take charge, or there were more of us, or . . . something. But we're it. And if we can't work together, we have no hope at all."

Det inclined his head gracefully, accepting Anders's words, and for a few minutes, Anders thought he had solved at least one problem.

But then Ellukka left those adjusting the straps on Mikkel, to catch at Anders's arm and draw him aside. "Is it safe to leave the wolves here?" she asked quietly.

"What?" Anders said. "Yes, of course it's safe."

"You trust them?" she pressed.

Anders groaned. "Yes, I trust them," he said. "They stood up to the Fyrstulf for us. Ellukka, wolves are a *pack*. You can't imagine what it took for them to do that."

"Probably not," she admitted. "But they've had a whole night to think over what they did. Do they still feel the same way?"

"I trust them," Anders said. "And if you trust me, then you should as well."

She was quiet for a long moment, and then she nodded. But Anders wasn't completely sure he'd convinced her.

Finally the harnesses were ready. Anders stepped back out of the way as Rayna shot him a grin, dropping to a three-point crouch, resting one hand on the floor. An instant later she was growing too fast for the eye to follow, shifting her shape as her skin changed to a rich crimson, with highlights of darker bronze and glittering copper darting across her scales. Her wings unfurled and her tail lengthened and gave one cheerful flick, and she was her dragon self, looming above him.

She dipped her head as Anders pulled on her harness, and held still as he tugged at the weak spots they'd mended until he was satisfied they wouldn't snap in midair, sending him tumbling toward the ground below. But she was clearly impatient to be aloft and spread her wings properly, and after a minute she snaked her neck around so she could nudge at him with her nose. She might as well have spoken out loud—she was saying, "Let's go, hurry up!"

So he planted one foot on her forearm and grabbed hold of the leather straps, pulling himself up until he could take his place just above her shoulders, fastening himself in. As soon as he reached down to pat Rayna's neck and signal he was ready, she launched, wings spread, letting an updraft carry her away from their temporary home.

He tried to admire the dawn as they left Cloudhaven. The mist pooled like water amid the trees below, tinted golden by the rising sun. But it was hard to keep his mind off his troubles. Though he understood why it was so difficult for his friends to trust each other, he didn't have time for them to slowly come around. Things were far too urgent for that. He leaned into Rayna's comforting warmth, closing his eyes and trying to convince himself all would be well as her wings beat beneath him and the miles stretched out below.

But when Holbard eventually came into sight, Anders forgot all his worries about his friends.

The city was a scene of devastation.

The great outer walls were crumbling, the stones spilling onto the ground. Huge swaths of buildings had simply been flattened when the earth had shaken beneath them, especially near the Wily Wolf tavern, where the Snowstone had exploded, and around the huge cracks that had opened up in the ground as the lava pulled by the Sun Scepter had fought to free itself.

The wreckage of ships floated in the harbor, and small fires still burned in shops and homes and warehouses. The north and northeast gates in the city walls had collapsed completely, but lines of people streamed out of the west and northwest gates, carrying what they could in their arms.

The dragons kept their distance, circling down to

land well to the west of the city, where they had before. Everyone looked grim as Rayna and Theo shifted back to human shape, and they worked together to hide the harnesses in the bushes.

But even in the middle of his horror, Anders's stomach still managed to rumble, protesting its lack of breakfast. One more small problem to add to his big ones. It was going to be a long walk to the city, but there was nothing for it except to get moving.

They pushed through the tide of people streaming along the road. Up close the refugees were ragged and covered in dust, and Anders could see the shock in their dirty faces, eyes fixed straight ahead, gazes set on nothing in particular.

The children passed through the west gate, walking past the crumbled, ruined buildings lining Ulfarstrat toward Ulfar Academy. The great street itself was mostly clear, and they were able to dodge debris as they made their way along it.

"We can make it the rest of the way," said Lisabet. "You should get moving."

Though none of them much liked the idea, they had decided to split up, with Lisabet and Mikkel to explore the ruins of Ulfar for what they could find of the library, and Anders and Rayna to search for food and supplies for the group. They would meet at noon at the west gate or, if any of them were held up, that night where they had hidden the harnesses.

"If we're later than that," said Rayna grimly, "then you'll know we're in trouble."

It was a strange, scary experience, making their way through the streets of Holbard. As Anders and Rayna climbed over a big chunk of rubble, he realized that just now, seeing the city like this reminded him of his first time in the Ulfar uniform. He had gazed in the mirror and seen his face looking back out of somebody else's body, his hair cut short, his uniform too different from his street clothes. Only his eyes had seemed really the same. The rest had been unrecognizable.

Among the ruins he could see familiar glimpses of a shop sign here, the brightly painted wall of a house there, crumbled into rubble.

"We did this," he said quietly to his sister.

She looked across at him. "We didn't mean to," she replied.

But the defiance in her tone was mingled with something else that told him she was feeling the same way he was.

"We were trying to stop them killing the dragons," Rayna said. "And we did."

As if her words had summoned one of those very dragons, a shadow passed over them and glided on, seeming to jump this way and that as the ground beneath it rose and fell. It was a huge, dark-red dragon, at least fifty feet long. A member of the Dragonmeet, Anders was almost sure.

In the past, there had sometimes been rumors of dragons over Holbard, whispers or scary stories, and in his time at Ulfar he'd seen a dragon spy transform and flee for her life, but he'd never seen a dragon simply brazenly fly over the city in the middle of the day.

As it wheeled back in their direction once more, he and Rayna ducked into the shadow of someone's house. Broken beams stuck out of it like fingers reaching for the sky, and the twins' feet were planted firmly on a great spill of dirt and grass where the rooftop meadow above them had tumbled to the ground.

When the shadow moved on, Rayna shifted, ready to step back out into the street, but some instinct made Anders grab her and hold her still. A few moments later a pair of wolves came running past, loping down the street, dodging the debris. One slowed to a trot, then stopped completely. As its companion wheeled around to check on it, the first wolf lifted its head, sniffing the wind.

Panic jolted through Anders. He had been riding a

dragon just an hour before. The wolf would smell the dragon on him.

Then a man rose from the shadows. He drew his arm back and let loose a rock, sending it sailing straight at the wolves.

It struck one of them squarely on the haunches, and the wolf skipped away with an angry yelp. But though it snarled at the man and its companion growled, the two of them turned to lope away.

The man spotted Anders and Rayna where they were huddled against the side of the house. Rayna had her mouth open, and Anders was simply staring. All their lives, the Wolf Guard had patrolled Holbard, had protected its citizens and enforced the law. *Everybody* did what a wolf asked them to do. Anders couldn't believe he'd just seen someone throw a rock at one.

"They did this," the man said, pointing after the wolves, his voice quivering with anger. "Them and the dragons. The elementals did this to Holbard. What do they think this place is? Somewhere to play their games? Did they think of us at all? You two should get back to your parents. It's not safe."

Anders tried to speak, but he couldn't make his mouth work. Rayna grabbed ahold of his hand.

"We will," she promised, already starting to tug him

away. But Anders couldn't shake the man's words.

Did they think of us at all? he had said.

Anders knew the truth was that most of the elementals never had. Not during the battle, and not before it, and probably not since, except to wonder if the humans would still follow the commands of the wolves. His mood was grim as they set off down the broken street again.

The twins had hoped that the marketplace would be the best place to find food, and when they reached it, Anders was relieved to see that they had been right. Goods were spilling out of ruined and abandoned stalls with nobody to salvage them, and shops had been broken open by the earthquakes.

Anders usually worried about stealing, but this food would go bad before the real owners had the chance to retrieve it.

And, he thought darkly, *it's probably too late to worry about stealing after destroying the city.*

There were others picking over the ruins in search of a meal, so the twins hefted the empty bags they'd brought with them and joined the other scavengers.

A little while later, Anders was trying to stuff a wheel of cheese into the too-small opening of his bag when he heard a whisper.

"Psst! Anders!"

He straightened, wary, running his eyes over the ruins and debris around him, trying to find the source of the voice.

A pasty-white face with a shock of black hair was peeking out from behind the jagged half of a wall. Anders recognized the grubby features, but he didn't know the boy's name. He was sure he was one of Jerro's little brothers, though. Jerro was another boy from the streets, and the day Anders had made his transformation, Jerro had helped him escape the wolves by swapping cloaks with him. Anders had repaid the favor ten times over by rescuing Jerro and his brothers from the roof of a burning house during the great fire at the port.

A thought suddenly surfaced to tug at him. Just after they'd escaped the battle, Sakarias had something to tell him about that fire. It was said to be dragonsfire—it looked like dragonsfire—but Anders wasn't so sure. He made a note to ask Sakarias again.

But just now, Jerro's brother was staring at him, sizing him up. Anders moved closer, but not too close.

"Where's Jerro?" he asked quietly.

"I don't know," the boy admitted. "Can we trust you?"

"Of course," Anders replied.

Everyone looked out for themselves on the streets, but none of them would ever put another in danger.

"You were on wanted posters," the boy pointed out.

"That has nothing to do with—you can trust us," Anders insisted. "Are you all right?"

"No," the boy admitted. "Pellarin's hurt. We need help."

Jerro was about the twins' age, and this boy looked perhaps a year younger, so Pellarin must be the smallest brother.

Anders signaled to Rayna, who was emerging from the ruins of a bakery with a huge fruit tart in her arms. It had about as much chance of fitting into her bag as the cheese wheel had into Anders's, but it did look delicious. She made her way over to him, and he told her what had happened.

"What's your name?" she asked the boy.

"Sam," he replied. "Will you help us?"

"Of course," she replied simply. "Show us where he is."

Sam spoke quietly as they made their way to the place he had Pellarin hidden. "We haven't seen Jerro since the battle," he said. "He'd gone over to Pila Square to get some scraps from the baker there, and he never came back. We had to leave where we were hiding because the roof fell in, so now he doesn't know where to look for us."

Anders's breath caught uncomfortably in his throat. That was a whole day ago now. Jerro wouldn't leave his

brothers alone that long if he could help it. He'd be searching if he possibly could. So where was he?

Sam had managed to hide his little brother in the stable of an inn, propping him up in a pile of hay. Pellarin
was covered in dust, and his leg was carefully positioned
on a saddle, bloodied and bruised.

"I'm almost sure it's broken," Sam said.

"Hello," said Pellarin. "Aren't you criminals?"

"Beggars can't be choosers," Rayna told him, her tone
deliberately cheerful.

"The leg is getting worse," Sam said quietly, and Pellarin didn't deny that.

Anders exchanged a long, long look with his sister.
They couldn't leave the boys here. The code of the street
said that you helped each other. Anders would want Jerro's
brothers to help Rayna if she were the one who was hurt.
And anyway, he simply couldn't do it.

A small nod told him that she felt the same way. "We'll
need to make a stretcher," she said with a sigh.

"Where are you going to take us?" Sam asked.

"To where we're staying," Anders replied. "It's, uh . . .
outside the city. We have a medic there, sort of." He
thought of Viktoria, who was at least *training* to be a medic
among the wolves. She had to know more than they did
about what to do with Pellarin's leg.

Rayna gave him a meaningful look and cleared her throat.

"Oh," said Anders. "Yes. I'm not going to lie, there are dragons where we're hiding. But—"

He was immediately drowned out in a wave of protests from both Sam and Pellarin, who tried to prop himself up on his elbows, then collapsed back, wincing in pain.

"They're on our side," Anders said as soon as he could get a word in edgewise. "Trust me. I helped you get out of the fire, didn't I? I'm not going to lead you into danger now."

"And what else are you going to do?" Rayna asked. "Stay here?"

Sam studied them for a long moment, worried, and Anders knew he was asking himself what Jerro would do.

But then Pellarin shifted restlessly, wincing again, and the decision was made.

"All right," he said. "Let's make that stretcher. And if you're lying about this, I'll never forgive you."

"If we're lying, you'll have been eaten by a dragon," Rayna pointed out. "But you won't be."

"What about Jerro?" Pellarin asked. "He might come back, and he won't know where to find us."

"We'll try to look for him," Rayna assured him, her tone turning serious.

Anders wished things were different, and that she didn't have to say *try*.

"We should hurry," is all he said, "or we'll miss meeting the others at noon, and we'll have to carry him all the way to the harnesses by ourselves."

So while Rayna ran back to the market to finish gathering as much food as she could, promising to stuff the backpacks until they couldn't take another ounce, Anders and Sam made up a stretcher. They took two brooms and then raided the stable, stringing sets of reins between them to support Pellarin and laying sacks on top of those.

When Rayna returned, she inspected their handiwork and nodded her approval.

"If only the horses themselves had stuck around," she said. But she helped the boys transfer Pellarin onto the stretcher, and she and Anders took the first turn at carrying him. Sam trailed a few steps behind, clearly still not sure he was making the right decision.

As they turned for the west gate, Anders hoped that Lisabet and Mikkel had found what they needed in the library. Coming here had been a big risk—they couldn't afford to come back too many times.

They were nearly at the west gate when a big man in a dirty black cloak stepped out to block their way. "What's in those bags?" he asked roughly.

Behind them, Sam squeaked, and when Anders turned his head, he saw a blond woman with long, curling hair and a dark-blue coat and trousers standing behind them, blocking their way back. Her clothes were fancy—like she'd had money before the city had collapsed.

"It's none of your business what's in our bags," Anders said, his words much braver than he felt. He only hoped his voice sounded steady. "It belongs to us."

"Where are your parents?" asked the woman. But there was no kindness in her voice—she wasn't wondering why the children were out alone, or if anyone was taking care of the boy who was so clearly hurt. Anders could tell that as far as she was concerned, the absence of their parents just presented an opportunity.

"They're not far away," Rayna replied immediately. "Do you know who this is?" She pointed at Pellarin, whose eyes widened.

"Why should we know who some brat is?" the man asked.

"I thought not," Rayna said, "or you'd be out of our way already."

Anders tried to give her a warning look. Rayna was always talking their way out of situations, and sometimes it worked, but sometimes you ended up on the dais in front of half of Holbard, grabbing the Staff of Hadda and turning into a wolf.

But there was no stopping her. "This is the mayor's son," she said, "and the mayor is not going to like it if you mess with us getting him to a doctor."

"*Him?*" the man said, his voice rich with disbelief.

"Well, he's not usually so dirty," Rayna pointed out, exasperated.

Anders looked back at the woman. "If you follow this road," he said, pointing, "you'll end up at the market. There's a lot of food there."

Go on, he silently urged her. *I'm giving you a way to get what you want. Just take it.*

The woman paused, then nodded at her partner. "Let's go," she said.

The man walked past Anders, Rayna, Sam, and Pellarin on the stretcher. He took his time sauntering, as if to make sure they knew that he could stop if he wanted, that he could do anything that he wanted. He took a good, long look at Pellarin, who closed his eyes.

The wolf in Anders wanted to growl in the back of his throat. But he kept himself quiet.

As soon as the man and the woman were gone, the

children hurried on down the uneven road, heading for the gate.

"Come to think of it," said Rayna, puffing now, "where *is* the mayor?"

"Out at the camps, probably," Sam said.

"The camps?" Anders asked.

"They're outside the city," Sam supplied, "where nothing can fall off a building and land on top of you. Most people are going there. They've gone out the west and northwest gates and they're sheltering along the banks of the Sudrain River."

"Have they gone to Upper Vadobrun?" Rayna asked, no doubt imagining the lay of the land from her now-usual view high above it, and thinking of the village to the north of the city.

"Too far," Sam replied. "That's nearly a full day's walk, and it's too small anyway. Nowhere for us all to fit."

"But there are still people left in here," Anders protested. "The mayor can't just leave, not to a camp and not to a village."

"Not *many* people," said Sam with a shrug, "and they don't care about people like us. Who'd miss us if we were gone?"

"Us," said Anders. "We would miss you."

But he knew that Sam was right. The man who had thrown the rock at the Wolf Guard had been right. The elementals never thought about the people who were caught up in their troubles, just like the people of Holbard had never thought about the street children.

But Anders would. He would help Sam and Pellarin, and he would find Jerro.

He would help everyone.

Somehow.

CHAPTER THREE

IT TOOK MORE THAN A LITTLE WRANGLING TO GET
the stretcher suspended underneath Mikkel, but they
managed it in the end. When he and Rayna touched
down at Cloudhaven with Anders, Lisabet, Sam, and Pellarin, there was a surprise waiting for all of them.

Ellukka and Theo had returned safely from Drekhelm,
but they weren't alone. Waiting with them on the landing
pad were three more of the Finskólars. Quiet and thoughtful Bryn, their languages expert—whom Anders had been
wishing were here only the night before—was standing
beside Ellukka. A little way behind them, staring up at the
sky, was the absentminded Isabina, the Finskól's resident
mechanics expert. Waiting with his usual broad grin, his
golden curls lit up by the sunset, waving enthusiastically,
was Ferdie, who was studying medicine at the Finskól. Or
had been studying medicine, perhaps, if he was here. Were

the three of them even Finskólars anymore, if they'd left Drekhelm?

"What happened?" asked Anders as he slid down from Rayna's back. He reached up to help Sam down so they could start pulling off Rayna's harness. "I mean, it's good to see you, hello, but also what happened?"

He shot a quick, inquiring glance at Ellukka, though, and she flashed him a smile, confirming it was indeed good news.

When Mikkel and Theo had made their escape from Drekhelm a couple of days before, it had been the Finskólars who had gotten in the way of the Dragonmeet pursuing them. What they hadn't known at the time was whether their classmates were tripping up the adults and buying the boys time to run for it accidentally or on purpose. The presence of Bryn, Isabina, and Ferdie answered that question now.

"What?" said Ferdie. "You thought that Leif was going to give us all those talks about loyalty and none of them were going to sink in? You're Finskólars. You need us. We're here." He paused, craning his neck to look over at where Lisabet and Theo were carefully unstrapping Pellarin's stretcher from Mikkel's harness. "And I think," he continued, "I'm needed over there."

"He's hurt his leg," Lisabet called. "Probably broken it."

Sam and the dragons crowded around to help untie the stretcher and carry it across the landing pad toward the entrance hall. Anders jogged ahead of them, to where the wolves were emerging from the arch. Judging by their expressions, they hadn't realized that extra dragons were waiting for them outside.

"It's all right," he said once he was in earshot. "They're friends of ours. They can help us. Viktoria, the tall guy over there is Ferdie. He's studying medicine at the dragons' Finskól. You and he have a patient waiting."

Viktoria simply nodded and hurried past him—he didn't doubt she was suspicious, but a patient was a patient.

They all made their way inside, Viktoria, Sam, Ellukka, and Ferdie carrying Pellarin's stretcher. A wolf, a human, and two dragons working together—that wasn't something Anders would have imagined a few days ago.

It was only when they all neared the fireplace that Anders realized there were bags and crates stacked in the shadows beside it.

"We brought supplies," Bryn said, falling into step with him. She was a full head taller than Anders, and more muscular too, her sleek black hair and light-brown skin showing her ancestors must have come from Ohiro. There was something calm about her presence that he appreciated right now. "Ellukka and Theo said you didn't

45

have anything," she continued. "There's food, bedding, and Ferdie's medical kit, and Isabina brought a whole lot of tools that . . . well, I don't know what they're for. But she seemed confident." Bryn hesitated, then lowered her voice. "Anders, these wolves—they're safe, right? Are these the same ones who attacked Drekhelm?"

Anders looked at his packmates, who were matching the dragons, suspicious glance for suspicious glance.

"Yes," he admitted, "but they're my classmates. They thought Lisabet and I were being held prisoner."

He felt just a little tired at the idea of trying yet again to convince the wolves and dragons to trust each other. But then he looked over at where Viktoria and Ferdie were in quick, quiet conversation, leaning over Pellarin and already unpacking Ferdie's medical supplies, and he felt a small flicker of hope. Perhaps it could be done. Eventually.

A few minutes later they had everything inside, and everyone except the two medics and Pellarin gathered around the fire. They set themselves up nearby, where they could still join the conversation. Bryn and Jai had broken open one of the boxes and were handing around slices of thick, sticky fruit bun with frosting on top that stuck to Anders's fingers. They cut up Rayna's giant fruit

46

tart as well—she'd made Sam hold it the whole way home, refusing to leave it behind even though it wouldn't fit into their bags.

The food seemed to make a difference to everyone's morale, and Anders noticed there were fewer suspicious looks just at this particular moment. Unless he counted Sakarias, whose attention was focused on Ferdie—he didn't seem to like him talking quite so much with Viktoria.

"Let's take turns reporting," Anders said. "Sak, you go first. Anything happen here while we were gone?"

Sakarias turned his attention away from the medical team and shook his head. "All quiet here," he said. "Cloudhaven behaved itself. We thought we heard something somewhere inside the mountain, but then it stopped. And not all of us heard it. It might have been nothing."

Anders thought of the room full of mechanical structures he'd seen the night before. Maybe it had been one of the machines?

"I guess we'll keep our ears open," Lisabet suggested. "It might have been nothing, but it might have been something."

Then she, Anders, Rayna, and Mikkel reported on their trip to Holbard. Lisabet showed the others the big stack of books she and Mikkel had retrieved from the ruins of the Ulfar library.

"With any luck, there'll be something in here that helps us understand how Cloudhaven was built, and how to control it," Lisabet said. Her face was even paler than usual, and her words were clipped. She'd loved their school library, and Anders could tell how much it had hurt her to see it destroyed.

Anders and Rayna explained how they knew Sam and Pellarin, and they talked about what they had seen in the city. Sam joined in for that, and all the wolves' faces grew graver and graver as they came to understand just how serious things were back at their home.

"So almost everyone's outside the city in the camps now?" Mateo asked. "What about the wolves? Are they there too? If everyone's blaming them, like you said, is it safe for them to be where everyone else is?"

Sam shrugged. "I haven't been to the camps," he said. "I don't know if they're with everyone else. I think, if they're in a pack, the wolves will be safe wherever they are. People might blame one or two wolves, but nobody's going to confront the whole Wolf Guard."

"The wolves aren't the only ones with problems, though," Anders said quietly. He tried to explain what else he'd seen, that as the dragons and wolves had fought over Holbard, and over who would control the climate of Vallen, they had left every human in the city without a roof over their head, without any certainty about what would come tomorrow.

Then it was Ellukka and Theo's turn. They'd come back from Drekhelm with all the books Theo had wanted, but they explained how they'd managed to bring back three Finskólars as well.

"The class was taking turns keeping a lookout," Ellukka said.

"Well, *some* of the class," Theo corrected her.

Anders exchanged a glance with his sister, and he knew they were both wondering what would have happened if the Finskólars who *didn't* like them had been keeping a lookout instead.

"It was actually quite interesting," Isabina said, rousing herself from her current daydream. Her brown curls were as wild as ever, and as usual, she had a smudge of black grease from one of her inventions on her white cheek. "There were some fascinating cloud formations. I was just classifying them, when suddenly I saw Theo drop out of the bottom of one. So I transformed straight away and flew up to join him. We all landed a little way down the mountain, which was safer, and swapped stories."

"Then she came to find us," Bryn said. "It's a mess

back at Drekhelm. Half the Dragonmeet is blaming the other half of the Dragonmeet for what happened at Holbard. Some of them still think that you were fighting for the dragons, and they're waiting for you to come back and join them again. Others are sure that you were never fighting for the dragons, and that you're traitors who need to be caught."

"How's your father, Ellukka?" Lisabet asked. There was nothing but concern in her voice, and Anders admired her compassion, as he had many times before.

Ellukka's father, Valerius, had mistrusted Anders and Lisabet from the first time he'd met them. He had made their time at Drekhelm difficult over and over again, but he still loved Ellukka with all his heart. In the battle over Holbard, he had been injured protecting her.

"He's all right," Ellukka replied, her relief written all over her face. "He's still injured, but he's going to be fine." She glanced down at the last pieces of her bun, her voice dropping. "He'd probably be finer if he knew I was all right too," she admitted.

There was nothing anyone could say to make her feel better, and after a moment, Theo spoke, although gently. "Leif's wondering where we are as well," he said.

"That's right," Bryn agreed. "To be completely honest, I think he *wanted* us to find you and join you. Only the fact that none of the Dragonmeet can agree with any of the others—as though they ever did—has stopped them from doing something stupid."

"How can we be sure he wanted that?" Theo asked.

"Well," Bryn replied, grinning, "most of these supplies were stacked in his office, and he left the door wide open. Then he called Ferdie, Isabina, and me in to talk to us. He said at a time like this, it was important not to stop learning, and gave us a book he thought we might find interesting. It was all about a small group of warriors who managed to win a war against a much larger army."

"It would make sense," Anders said. "He's the one who sent us off after the Sun Scepter in the first place, more or less. He never actually *said* we should do something, but he sort of . . . made it obvious."

The conversation drifted on, and those who had come to Cloudhaven first explained to the others about their difficulty getting inside. The afternoon was already growing chilly, and a cold wind was sweeping in through the open archway that led out to the landing pad.

"We *have* to get the rest of you properly inside, past the wooden door," Rayna said. "There's hundreds of rooms in there. Some of them must be bedrooms, and we'll be able to get warm as well. And we'll be much safer if anyone shows up looking for us."

Viktoria and Ferdie finished with Pellarin, who was dozing lightly.

"We've cleaned his wounds and seen to his leg," Viktoria said. "Ferdie's supplies are very good."

"So's your splinting technique," Ferdie replied as he accepted a piece of fruit tart from Sam. *At least,* thought Anders, *the medics are getting on. And maybe even doing a better job together than they could have apart.*

"Pellarin will sleep for now," Viktoria said. "It would be much better if he could rest somewhere more comfortable. That's not possible though, is it?"

"No," said Anders. "Really, we have the same challenges as we did before, and maybe some extra. We need to find a way inside Cloudhaven, so we're safe. Then we need to find a way to make everyone else in Vallen safe. We need to clean up the messes we've made. It doesn't matter that we were trying to stop the Snowstone from killing the dragons and harming the humans. We're still responsible for what happened to Holbard. So from finding Jerro right up to figuring out what to do about the city, we . . ."

"We need to fix everything," Rayna agreed.

The thought of climbing a mountain that high was enough to silence everyone.

Eventually, it was Jai who broke the silence, rising to

their feet. "Well," they said, "if we're going to do all that, a sticky fruit bun might not be enough. We should probably start with dinner."

So Jai and Det got to work bossing around assistants and starting work on a meal, and Anders and Rayna headed inside Cloudhaven proper one more time.

Anders's job was to go to the wall that concealed the way to their mother and copy the words down for Bryn to try and translate. Rayna's job—which he didn't envy—was to try and draw at least some of the designs inside the mechanical room for Isabina, in the hope that she might recognize them or understand how to work them. If only Sakarias had been able to go inside—he could bring anything to life with his pencil. Instead, he tried to explain techniques to Rayna for observing one piece of the room at a time and sketching what she saw. The stronghold seemed willing to light up more than one path for them at once, and he was grateful for that.

The third path it had shown them—the one that had led directly to their own feet when they had asked it to help them bring the others inside—neither of them had any idea how to investigate. They simply had to hope that Lisabet, Theo, and their helpers would find something in the books they'd retrieved.

Anders sat in front of the rock wall and put his mind

to copying down the words. It wasn't easy—Anders had to concentrate extra hard to understand most writing, and when all the words were in a different language, some of them even containing different letters than the ones he was used to, the task certainly didn't get any easier. He checked and double-checked and triple-checked each letter and each word to make sure all his copying was right.

He was about halfway through, and starting to daydream a little bit about what might be coming for dinner, when he thought he heard a noise just around the corner. It was like one rock clicking against another. Then there was a soft shuffle and another click.

"Rayna?" he called. "You can't be done already. No way."

When there was no answer, he lifted his head and looked along the hallway. There was nobody there.

"Rayna?" he tried again, raising his voice.

Then a third time, much louder. "Rayna! Are you there?"

He heard a very distant shout of reply. "What?"

No question. She wasn't close. Not just around the corner. She was still off at the mechanical room.

"Never mind," he yelled, and studied the corner again, his pulse kicking up. "Cloudhaven," he said quietly, "is somebody else here?"

Nothing happened.

He considered his words and tried a different way.

"Cloudhaven, could you lead me to someone who's here right now, who's not me and not Rayna?"

The lights dimmed, and then the path that he had come to expect lit up once more. But it didn't lead away toward the corner where he had heard the noise. It led straight into Drifa's wall.

"Well, I already knew that," he muttered.

Still, he was sure he'd heard something. So he levered himself to his feet and made his way along the hallway up toward the corner, silently wondering what, exactly, he was going to do if it turned out there *was* an enemy there.

But when he reached it, trying to walk as though he had confidence, standing tall, shoulders squared, there was nobody there at all.

"Guess I was hearing things, Cloudhaven," he said. "And I guess now I'm talking to a giant pile of rocks in the sky. This is going well."

With a sigh, he turned and walked back to his work, picking up his notebook so he could finish off the second half.

When he was eventually done, he took the long way out, checking in on his sister first. She was muttering feverishly to herself, and he wasn't sure how to tell her that her picture looked like nothing so much as a cobweb made by a demented spider, the scratchy lines that were meant to depict wires spinning out in every direction to every corner of the page.

"Looks good," he said instead, and patted her on the shoulder. "Do you need a hand?"

She waved him off. "I'll see you out there."

So Anders headed back out to where his friends were hopefully researching and cooking and checking on their patient.

They were indeed all hard at work. Jai and Det were commanding a group of wolves, dragons, and Sam the human, pulling together a meal that smelled absolutely amazing.

Lisabet and Theo had all the others helping them. They already had a dozen books open, and were crawling back and forth across the floor, comparing paragraphs and arguing with each other in quiet voices. They didn't look like they'd had any breakthroughs yet, but if they were stopping to read parts of the books, Anders hoped that meant they might be relevant.

Lisabet had always been famous among the wolves for her love of the library, and Theo had been studying research and archiving at the Finskól. Ellukka had been studying storytelling, and Mikkel history, and the two of them were also nose-deep in books, hunting for information about how Cloudhaven worked.

He stood for a moment before he approached the little camp, just watching. Mateo was holding three books open at once for the others, one with each of his hands and one with a foot. At least they were all talking to each other—wolf, dragon, and human—and working together a little bit. It wasn't much, but it was something.

Anders delivered his notebook to Bryn, who promptly buried herself in it, ignoring him and everyone else. Anders was no scholar, though, so as Bryn settled herself down by the fire to begin work on the arduous translation, he presented himself to the cooks to see what he could do.

It was much later that night, after food and a little more work, when they all reconvened to talk about what they should do next.

"I think we're starting to get an idea of how this place works," Lisabet said, "but it won't be fast, and we can already tell there are going to be some dead ends. Dragons have been forbidden from coming here for as long as we can remember. If Drifa came here, then she was breaking the rules. Cloudhaven's ancient, and so are the books about it. Only a few of us can work at once—there aren't enough books for everyone to research."

"Is there anything the rest of us can do?" Sakarias

asked. "I don't just want to sit here and do nothing, not with everything that's happened."

Sam was sitting beside Pellarin, who had woken long enough to have a small meal and was now fast asleep again. Anders saw Sam shift, as though he wasn't sure whether he should speak or not.

"We could . . . ," Sam began, then paused. His black hair was falling into his eyes, desperately in need of a cut, and there was nowhere to wash at Cloudhaven apart from the ice-cold water in the tiny sink of their one little washroom. ("We're lucky someone thought about whether visitors might need bathroom facilities at all," Sakarias had pointed out.) So Sam still had dirt daubed across his cheeks, more smeared than cleaned by his efforts at tidying himself up. He looked thin, but to Anders, he didn't look young. Anders knew how much experience Sam had had on the streets. He knew Sam was used to fending for himself. In a way, Sam was like Anders and Rayna, older in experience than any of the wolves or dragons here.

"Go on," said Anders when it seemed no one else had noticed Sam thinking about speaking. "Did you have an idea, Sam?"

Sam nodded, and the others turned their attention to him. "I was thinking about the camps," he said. "Almost everyone from Holbard is outside the city, in the camps, but they must be a mess. They won't have any shelter. I'm not even sure if they'll have enough food. How could they possibly have found a way to look after that many people this quickly?"

"And your brother might be there," Rayna pointed out. "Jerro must be somewhere."

"Maybe," Sam agreed, "and I want to find him. I want to find him very badly. But there's more to it than that. Maybe you could help the Holbard refugees. There must be a lot of injuries. You have people here who have trained as medics."

To Anders's surprise, it was Viktoria who spoke up. "*We* have people trained as medics," she corrected him. "You're here too, Sam. You're one of us. And I think we should do it. Pellarin will be okay tomorrow without us."

Sitting beside her, Ferdie nodded, his usually cheerful face grave. "We're doing what we can," he said, "but mostly, Pel just needs to sleep. And wait."

"Then let's go to the town camp," Anders said. "Maybe we'll find Jerro. Maybe we'll find people who need medics. Maybe we'll find some other way we can help. I want to do something, not just sit here."

"I'll take you," Ellukka offered.

"And I'll come too," Rayna said.

"Viktoria and I can both come," Ferdie said, and Sakarias looked at him just a moment too long.

And so it was decided. In the morning, they would head to the camps.

They settled down to a much more comfortable rest, thanks to the quilts and blankets that Ferdie, Bryn, and Isabina had brought with them.

As he had the night before, Anders stared at the embers as he drifted off to sleep. This time, he felt a little more hopeful. He didn't know what tomorrow would bring, but he was ready to find out.

CHAPTER FOUR

THE NEXT DAY, THE SIX OF THEM—ANDERS, Rayna, Ferdie, Viktoria, Ellukka, and Sam—made the long walk from their safe landing place into the camp outside Holbard.

It felt a little like the slow horror of coming into Holbard proper and beginning to understand how much damage had been done. But if anything, the town camp shocked Anders more. It was strung out along the banks of the Sudrain River, perhaps an hour's walk from the ruins of Holbard. Seeing the state of it now, he understood why nobody had made it as far as the village of Upper Vadobrun. He could hardly believe they'd made it this far.

The camp was chaos. Nothing was laid out in a way that made sense, salvaged belongings strewn around like debris from a shipwreck. The grass had already been trampled into mud, and everything was dirty. People had made shelters from whatever they could, stringing up cloaks or sheets of canvas, leaning salvaged doors and planks against each other, or simply sleeping out in the mud and in the open, piling their belongings together and guarding them carefully.

The faces around Anders were mean, worried, and pinched. They were the faces of people who didn't have much, and knew what they had wouldn't last very long. Everyone was looking out for themselves, and everyone was keeping an eye on their neighbors.

What he didn't see was any sign of the wolves, anywhere.

"They must be camping somewhere else," Viktoria murmured. "But the wolves know *how* to camp. We go out on excursions as part of our training. They could help here."

"Only if they're wanted," Ellukka said, "and I don't think they are."

"What's that up ahead?" Rayna asked, pointing as the top of what looked like a big tent came into view.

They made their way toward it through the crowd, moving slowly to avoid attracting attention. After all, Anders, Lisabet, and Rayna had been on wanted posters all around the city not so long ago. Nobody was paying attention now, though—the hoods of their cloaks were disguise enough. They stayed together, trying not to look too hard at anyone, just in case it was taken as a sign that they wanted to steal their belongings.

The place Rayna had seen did indeed turn out to be a huge tent. It was the only proper one in the camp, as far as Anders could tell, and out in front of it the mayor of Holbard himself sat on a real chair at a real table—both of those were also in short supply—speaking to a dirty man who was the first in a very, very long line.

The mayor was not dirty. The mayor was wearing his gold chain of office and clean clothes. Anders recognized him from all the times he had seen him stand beside Sigrid, the Fyrstulf, on the dais during the monthly Trial of the Staff. But even if he had not known the mayor by sight, it would have been clear to him that this man was in charge. He was surrounded by several members of Vallen's parliament and seemed to be taking requests or complaints. It didn't seem like he was doing anything about them, apart from occasionally gesturing for one of his companions to write something down, and everyone who left the front of the line walked away crestfallen, occasionally glancing back, as if they weren't quite sure what had just happened.

"Okay," said Rayna, "I think we should split up. Ferdie and Viktoria—and maybe you, Ellukka—you should go see who you can help. Maybe there's some kind of hospital here, somewhere people are going to get treatment."

"What about you?" Ellukka asked.

"Anders, Sam, and I need to take a look around here," Rayna said.

Anders knew exactly what she was thinking. "This is the only place anyone has anything to take," he said. "Nobody from the street would ever take something from those other people, the ones camping under their coats. We all know what it's like not to have anything. But here . . ."

"The mayor and his clean clothes are fair game," Sam finished for him.

"Right," Anders agreed. "And that means Jerro might be somewhere around here."

"He'd look for prime pickpocketing territory," Sam agreed. "And so might other people we know."

In his heart, Anders wasn't so sure they'd find Jerro—it was hard to imagine him pickpocketing when he could be looking for Sam and Pellarin—but he didn't want to say so out loud.

"This is also where we'll get the best gossip," Rayna said, clapping Sam a little too hard on the shoulder. Anders suspected she shared his worry about what might have happened to Jerro, but they had to try their best.

"All right," Viktoria agreed. "We'll come back this way in an hour, or at least one of us will, to see what's going on."

Viktoria and Ferdie took off, with Ellukka to keep lookout for them. Anders, Rayna, and Sam cast their eye over the scene before them, taking their time, slow and thoughtful, making sure they had the lay of the land before they committed themselves to anything.

This is just like being back in the city, Anders told himself. *You've done this a million times.*

And, of course, he had. Countless times, he and Rayna had sat on the edge of a roof, looking at the square below, scouting out every corner of it, making sure they knew who was there and what was where before they committed to any course of action. He had no doubt Sam had done the same thing with Jerro and Pellarin just as many times.

"I'd like to get inside that tent," Rayna murmured beside him with her usual audacity. "That's where the good stuff will be. And there are a lot of people out here who need it."

"We'd need better clothes," Sam pointed out, "or, at least, a much better cloak."

The two of them fell into quiet discussion about whose cloak might possibly be stolen, and Anders let them talk as he kept looking over the scene.

He studied the mayor and each of the politicians in turn, then began to study the attendants around them. What sort of people were they? Did they understand that everyone around them had nothing, while they had food and clean clothes? Did they care, if they knew?

His gaze shifted past a tall, heavyset man wearing glasses, and then abruptly flicked back to him.

He was much taller and much broader than Anders. He had dark-brown skin, black hair, and a black beard, neatly trimmed. His glasses had thick, square frames. His trousers were gray, and they might almost have been the same color as an Ulfar uniform. His shirt was a dark green, still clean, neatly tucked in. He wore an amulet at his neck, though he'd tucked it inside his shirt, where it was mostly hidden.

He looked like he belonged with the people all around him. Except he was far more serious than any of them.

And Anders knew who he was.

"Rayna," he whispered, tugging at her arm.

"I'm just saying," she said to Sam, "when you go for the ones with the buttons, it might look easier, but once you tug the edge of the cloak—"

"Rayna!"

"What?"

Then, before he had a chance to reply, she followed his gaze and went completely still.

The man standing over by the tent was their uncle Hayn, a teacher at Ulfar Academy, a famous artifact designer, and perhaps the person Anders wanted to see most in the world right now. Hayn had helped them get their hands on their mother's map. Had managed to get their augmenters to them, even after he'd been arrested. Hayn had always been on their side, trying to help them and protect them.

Carefully, Anders began to walk a slow circuit around the edge of the gathering, forcing himself to move at a regular pace so nobody would pay any special attention to him. Rayna was by his side, and Sam a few steps behind.

They were ten feet away when Hayn saw them, and he didn't have nearly as much practice as they did at playing it cool in tricky situations. He started, then broke into a run, closing the gap in three big strides and gathering each of them up in one arm, lifting them clean off their feet. Rayna squeaked, and Anders didn't even have enough air to do that. But luckily, their uncle set them down after just a few moments.

"Careful," Sam whispered from behind them, "someone will notice you."

Hayn looked up, white teeth flashing in a quick grin.

"The one thing nobody notices around here right now is a reunion," he said. "They're happening all the time. My name is Hayn. You must be a friend of my niece and nephew's."

He held out his hand to shake, and Sam stared at it for a long moment, before Rayna gave a tiny, encouraging nod.

Very carefully, as though his own hand might snap off, Sam shook. "Sam," he said uncertainly.

"Pleasure to meet you, Sam," Hayn said, just as if the introduction had been perfectly normal. "Come on, you three, let's find somewhere private, and we can talk."

He led them around the back of the big tent to a couple of pale square patches in what was left of the grass.

"Huh," he said. "There were crates to sit on here a few hours ago. I suppose someone salvaged them for some shelter."

So instead they stood while they talked.

"I'm so relieved to see you," Hayn said. "I had no idea if either of you were okay. I thought if there was any chance that you'd come to the camp, you'd come here, so I hung around and tried to blend in."

"You thought we'd come where the people were richer and the pickings were best?" Rayna asked, looking a little insulted, though that was in fact exactly what they had been thinking.

"No," Hayn replied, with much more faith in them than Anders felt they deserved. "This is where the decisions are being made. I thought you'd want to know what was happening."

"And we thought you'd be with the wolves," Anders admitted. "None of them are here."

"No, they've made a camp to the north," Hayn replied. "Up past Vadobrun, where the Ulfar students camp when they go out overnight. You remember it?"

Anders nodded. He and Lisabet had seen the place the night before they'd stolen Fylkir's chalice and run away to Drekhelm to find Rayna. "There's nothing there," he said. "Just a cairn with a few supplies, and the river."

"The wolves don't need much," Hayn replied. "They've trained for this. And they're not welcome among the citizens of Holbard, any more than I'm welcome among the wolves. You know I was locked up before the battle, because Sigrid suspected I was dragging my feet on finding her an augmenter for the Snowstone. I wasn't going back and giving them a chance to lock me up again. Not until I knew whether the two of you were safe."

"I don't even know what to ask first," Anders admitted. "What's happening with the wolves? What's happening here?"

"The wolves are doing all right," Hayn replied. "They

salvaged supplies from Holbard and marched out to make a camp. Sigrid is missing, and Professor Ennar is in charge."

Anders's heart skipped, then skipped again. It was good news that Ennar was in charge. When Hayn had been locked up and Sigrid had proclaimed Anders the enemy of the wolves, Ennar had had her doubts. She certainly wasn't on their side, but she might be willing to listen to Anders, if he could find the right words . . . and stop the rest of the wolves attacking long enough to begin a conversation.

But for Sigrid to be missing . . . he could already imagine Lisabet's face when she heard the news. Though she disagreed with her mother on almost everything, she still loved her.

And for his part, Anders was worried about where Sigrid was, and what she might be doing. He couldn't help thinking of all the rubble back in Holbard, and no matter what she had done, he hoped that she wasn't buried beneath it. If she was somewhere out there, though, on the loose, that would spell trouble for him and his friends.

He and Rayna quickly relayed everything that had happened since the last time they'd seen Hayn, with Sam adding details once they got to the part of the story that featured him. As they reached the end, their uncle wrapped an arm around each of their shoulders.

"You've both been so brave," he said.

"We've both been such failures," Anders replied. "Look at the city."

"That wasn't your fault," Hayn said firmly. "I don't know why the Snowstone or the Sun Scepter behaved the way they did. They're both powerful artifacts, but they shouldn't have caused this level of destruction." His voice dropped lower. "I have a horrible feeling . . . ," he began, then stopped.

Anders looked up at him. "A feeling about what?" he asked.

"They're both such old artifacts," Hayn replied. "I wasn't sure there was any chance they would work at all. I thought the augmenters were necessary."

Anders reached up to touch the augmenter that hung on a strap around his neck next to his Ulfar amulet, an artifact that made sure he still had his clothes when he turned from a wolf back into a human. The Ulfar amulet felt like a part of him now, and he had almost completely forgotten about the augmenter. In the midst of the battle, he and Rayna had made their way to Hayn's cell and found he had left a pair of augmenters behind, one for each of the twins.

"You mean the augmenters made the artifacts so powerful that they destroyed the city?"

"Maybe," said Hayn. "I honestly don't know."

"I don't suppose there's another artifact out there that we could use the augmenters on?" Anders asked wistfully. "Something that would rebuild everything?"

"I don't think it's that simple," Hayn replied, "but I can think of one thing you might be able to do with your augmenters. It's only a rumor, but even so . . ."

"What is it?" Anders was willing to try just about anything.

"This wall you told me about that leads to where Drifa is hidden," Hayn continued. "I don't know what it can possibly mean, but I have an idea about how you could find out."

He was digging through his pockets feverishly, and after a few moments, he produced a crumpled sheet of paper. It was thick, shot through with fibers, and as Anders looked at it more closely, he realized some of the fibers were very thin threads of metal. The paper itself was an artifact.

Hayn dug in his other pocket and produced a stub of a pencil, then gestured for Rayna to turn around and give him her back to lean on. He carefully inscribed a series of runes on each half of the paper, then folded it down the middle and tore along the fold, handing each of the twins one of the pieces.

"You still have your augmenters?" he asked.

Anders fished his out from where it hung down the front of his shirt. The little disc was covered in runes identical to the ones on Rayna's augmenter.

"Tonight," said Hayn, "I want you to take these pieces of paper and wrap them around the augmenters. It would be better if a dragonsmith forged the runes for you, but the paper's well made, and the runes I've designed are simple. I think it'll be enough, if the trick works at all. Find some way to fasten the paper firmly around the augmenters, so it won't fall off in the night. I've never actually seen it done, but if you're right and Drifa is somewhere in or around Cloudhaven, it might be possible to connect with her via your dreams. She might have some answers for you. If she's anywhere we can reach her, we need her badly right now. I don't think we've ever needed her more."

"We'll try tonight," Anders promised, already thinking of his spot beside the fire, itching to get back so he could go to sleep, and maybe find his mother.

But Rayna had caught something in Hayn's tone that Anders had missed. "You're coming back with us, right?" she asked.

Slowly, regretfully, Hayn shook his head. "Now I know you're safe, I'll see if I can get close to the wolves," he said. "It's not safe for me to talk to them yet, but if I spot an opportunity, I have to be there to take it. They can't keep themselves separate like this—I have to at least try to reason with them. The longer everyone's apart, the harder it will be to bring them back together. They're supposed to be protecting the humans—assuming the humans want anything to do with them. And what's the pack going to do, live out on the plains forever?" He shook his head again. "I don't know whether the humans *or* the wolves will be willing to talk, but I think it's a good idea to at least know what the wolves are doing."

He paused, though, pulling open his coat and reaching into one of the inside pockets. Now Anders could see that every time Hayn moved, his jacket swung—before he had left Ulfar, he must have stuffed it full of everything useful that he could carry.

He pulled out a little circular mirror of the sort Anders had seen the fancy citizens over on the west side of Holbard use. The mirror was inside a case that snapped closed to protect it. When you opened it, you could peer at your reflection and check . . . well, Anders didn't really know what people checked, but it always seemed important.

Since he'd gone to Ulfar, though, Anders had learned there were more uses for a mirror than inspecting yourself.

Hayn turned it around so the twins and Sam could get a good look at it, and Anders saw the runes engraved inside the lid.

"Have you seen a mirror like this?" Hayn asked. "The ones matched with this are exactly the same—the engravings are identical. You said Drifa had a workshop at Cloudhaven—I never knew that. But if the rest of the set is going to be anywhere, it will be there. One of them was my brother's." He spoke the last word lightly, but he, Anders, and Rayna all exchanged a long glance. Felix now meant a lot to all of them, and his loss had left a mark on each of them in their own way.

"It's a mirror for communication?" Anders asked.

His uncle nodded. "Felix and I used them, but his wasn't on him when he died, and it's never been opened since. If you can find it, we can easily stay in touch."

"We'll hunt for it," Rayna promised. "There's a lot of mess in the workshop. It could definitely still be there."

"If you can't find it," Hayn said, "I'll meet you back here at this time the day after tomorrow."

And with that plan made, none of them could afford to linger. They exchanged another long, long hug—Anders hadn't hugged someone so much larger than himself many times in his life. Or, he realized, perhaps at all, before he had met Hayn. He liked the way his uncle's arms wrapped him up tight, went all the way around him, and he rested his head against the big man's chest for a moment.

Then it was time to go.

"The day after tomorrow," Hayn promised. "And I'll be watching my mirror until then."

He slipped away into the crowd, and the three children watched him go.

When Anders looked back at the others, he saw the wistful expression on Sam's face as the other boy tracked Hayn until he was out of sight. Sam was wishing for his own reunion, of course.

"Well," said Anders, trying to sound cheerful, "we came here because we thought Jerro might be around, right? Because this is the smartest place to look if you want to pickpocket anybody. So let's look."

The three of them spread out a little to mingle with the crowd, making themselves unremarkable, keeping their hoods up and moving easily, exchanging glances to silently communicate. In a strange way, it actually felt good to do something so familiar.

And then a quarter of an hour later, the unexpected happened: they actually found Jerro. It was Rayna who spotted him, and she flicked one hand up in a discreet signal to draw the boys' attention to him.

Jerro was following one of the mayor's advisers, his hands in his pockets, his walk casual. His face had been scrubbed clean, but despite the loss of his usual dirt, he was unmistakable. Sam made a quiet noise of pure relief, and Anders felt like a huge weight had lifted off his shoulders.

"Well done, Jerro," approved Rayna. One of the first rules of pickpocketing was that you shouldn't stand out, so Jerro had cleaned himself up to fit in.

He was edging closer and closer to his mark, clearly preparing for a highly risky attempt at an in-transit lift, when he spotted his brother standing with the twins and stumbled abruptly. He fell straight into the man he was trying to steal from, and though the adviser turned around with a frown on his face, Jerro's quick and embarrassed apologies settled him down. With a gruff "No harm done," the man was on his way.

Jerro nodded at a giant, haphazard pile of firewood, and they hurried around to meet him behind it.

He didn't let Sam get a word out before he threw his arms around him, squeezing him tight.

"Where's Pel?" he asked urgently.

Sam wheezed and tried to reply, but it was left to Anders to speak.

"He's safe," he promised. "He hurt his leg, but he's back at our, uh . . . camp. We have medics who looked him over too. They said he'll be fine, but he can't go anywhere right now."

Sam thumped on Jerro's shoulder with one fist, and his big brother finally realized what was going on and released him.

Sam took a great, heaving breath and then grinned. "Sorry to spoil your lift," he said.

Jerro snorted, reaching into one pocket. "Spoiled what?" he asked, pulling out a handful of coins. "Just a different opportunity."

Sam laughed, and Anders felt himself grinning.

"You can come with us," Rayna said. "We'll take you to Pel. Is there anything else you brought out of the city that you need to get?"

Jerro opened his mouth to reply, paused, closed it again, opened it, and hesitated. "Um," he said eventually.

"Um?" Sam asked. "Jerro, you have to come. Pel can't leave. And anyway, it's better there. It's safe."

"It's not that," said Jerro. "It's just not that simple. I haven't been sticking around here for fun—if I could, I'd have been back in the city, hunting every second for Sam and Pel. Instead, I just had to hope they'd come here. You'd better follow me."

He led them through the camp once more, leaving the prosperous area and moving through the muddy parts where families were camped, cooking over fires, trying to gather together or protect the few things they had managed to take with them from the city.

And then they moved into the really poor part of camp, where the inhabitants simply huddled in their cloaks, without shelter or cooking fires.

It was there, clustered in the protection of a boulder, that Jerro showed them what the problem was. When he rounded the big rock, half a dozen small faces turned up toward him, like a nest full of baby birds waiting to be fed.

Except these weren't birds. These were children. All smaller than Anders and Rayna, all at least vaguely familiar from the streets of Holbard. Jerro had lost his two little brothers, but he had found all these children to protect, and protect them he had.

"I can't just leave them here," he said helplessly. "No one else will look after them. Some of the farmers from around the area have started coming into the camp with goods to sell. With the money I lifted, I can feed us for at least a day or two."

The twins exchanged a quick glance, communicating without words, as they almost always did. They both reached the same conclusion, and then Rayna spoke quietly.

"But what if they scream?" Rayna said quietly. "When they see, you know . . ." Her hands made a vague flapping motion. *When they see the dragons.*

"Well, Jerro's right," said Anders. "We can't just leave them here."

A skinny girl piped up from the cluster of children. "Jerro, are you going away?"

"Don't worry," said Rayna, "nobody's leaving anyone anywhere. It's time we met up with Viktoria and Ferdie and Ellukka. They're probably waiting for us by now—I'll go see. Anders, Sam, why don't you two take Jerro and the others out of the camp to where we . . ." She paused, because she clearly didn't want to say *landed* in front of Jerro and the others and give the game away. "To where we'll depart from," she settled on. "Wait for us there. That way, if anybody's going to scream or do anything stupid, they can do it where it's quiet."

Jerro looked like he had a lot of questions, but Sam squeezed his hand, and he kept them to himself for now, willing to trust his brother until they were away from the camp. He and his little troupe followed Anders and Sam out past the camp borders, clutching their few precious belongings in their arms.

It was a long walk out to the place where they were to meet the others, and Rayna, Viktoria, Ferdie, and Ellukka caught up with them before they reached it.

They waited until they were a good distance away, though—until it was inconvenient for anybody to try to run—before they explained exactly how they would be getting to Cloudhaven.

Some of the children took Rayna's, Ferdie's, and Ellukka's transformations into dragons more calmly than others, and there was a little screaming. But in the end, the older children managed to keep everybody together. Ferdie played the clown, leaning in and snorting hot breath at each of the children, letting them touch his nose and tickling them with the end of his tail. And, one by one, they began to relax.

Then, of course, they had a new problem: even though the children Jerro had rescued were small and skinny, together they all still weighed far more than any of the dragons had ever lifted before. Despite Ferdie being older, Ellukka was the biggest and strongest of the three, so she took more of the load than anyone.

Anders and Jerro carefully made sure each of the children was somehow tucked into her harness, arms or legs poking through, everyone under instructions to stay still and hold tight.

"That is a long way to fall," Jerro told them sternly, "so don't do it."

He was nervous as well, Anders could tell, but his big-brother instincts were hard at work, and he hid his own fear for the sake of his charges.

When Ellukka finally took off, Anders watched her struggling. It was as though she was clawing her way up through the air, gaining altitude very slowly, making her turns wide and careful. But she did it.

To his left, Ferdie and Viktoria took off with Sam hanging on behind her, and Anders helped Jerro climb up onto Rayna's back and sit behind him before they took off as well. Wondering what the others would make of their newest residents, they slowly began to wing their way toward Cloudhaven.

CHAPTER FIVE

THAT NIGHT, CLOUDHAVEN WAS BUSIER THAN IT had ever been before.

Ferdie and Viktoria were keeping a firm eye on Ellukka, making sure that she ate, and then ate a little more, to recover from her trip back.

Det and Jai were working with Sakarias and Bryn to feed many more mouths than they were used to, chopping and mixing, doling out food into bowls and passing them around—they had enough spoons and forks, but not quite enough bowls, and most of the children clustered around to share, scooping the food up eagerly.

Mateo, the biggest of the wolves, sat cross-legged with the smallest of the orphans in his lap, holding his bowl out in one large hand so she could dig her spoon in.

Lisabet sat quietly beside him, downcast. She had had no success with the books she was hoping would help her find a way inside Cloudhaven, and the news that her mother was missing had hit her hard. She didn't contribute to the conversation around the fire as the wolves, dragons, and other children all considered what they had learned that day.

"Hayn was right," Anders said. "We have to get the different groups to talk to each other. It's the only way anything will change. But I have no idea how we do that."

Surprisingly, it was Sakarias who shook his head. "That's not the way it goes," he said. "We don't talk to each other. We don't get along. And maybe there are reasons we've stayed apart."

Anders hadn't been prepared to hear Sakarias, of all people, say something so negative. But after a moment he remembered the way Sakarias had been looking at Ferdie and Viktoria every time they worked together. Sak and Viktoria had been friends and roommates for almost a full year at Ulfar. Wherever you found one, you always found the other.

Everyone was quiet for a moment, and then Ferdie broke the silence. He didn't sound offended—he was speaking in his usual, friendly tone, as if they were all getting along.

"I don't know, Sak. Do all wolves make stew like this?" he asked, holding up his bowl. "Because if they do,

I'm certainly willing to talk."

Sakarias made a soft grumbling sound, but Anders knew he was at least a little pleased—Ferdie had deliberately chosen the part of the meal that Sakarias had been in charge of.

But then, looking at his friend, Anders remembered something else. Speaking of not getting along . . .

"Sak," he said, "right after the battle at Holbard, you were going to tell me something about the fire down at the port, weren't you?"

Sakarias's expression grew serious. The fire at the port had been huge, swallowing up most of the houses that ringed the town square, and each of those several stories high. The flames had been white with gold sparks— dragonsfire—and the wolves had fought them valiantly.

It had been at that fire that Anders had rescued Jerro and his brothers from the roof.

He and Rayna had seen a fire just like this before, only it had been much, much smaller. They had watched a puppet show in one of the small squares of Holbard, and when the dragon puppets had flown in, the twins had marveled at how the flames seemed to be white. If the fire could be faked on such a small scale, Anders had thought after he saw the port fire, perhaps it could be done on a large scale as well.

He hadn't wanted it to be true, though.

"We went and took a look at it, like you asked," Sakarias said, his face grim. "It was the next morning. There was a lot of white ash there—it turned to powder when you touched it. And there were piles of this gray dust that seemed like it was made of metal. It didn't seem right. It wasn't what you usually see in the fireplace after a fire has burned itself out, but we couldn't work out what it was. Is that what you were expecting?"

"I'm not sure what I was expecting," Anders replied. "Do any of you dragons know if that's what's usually left behind after your flames?"

The dragons all shook their heads. "The flames look different from normal fire, but the ashes aren't any different," Ellukka said.

"Then why did *this* fire leave something different behind?" Lisabet asked.

"Um," said a voice. Sam had raised his hand. "I think we humans might have the answer to this one," he said. "While you wolves and dragons were off studying magic and battles, we were learning other things, and inventing some too. Anders, you're thinking of the puppet show at Trellig Square, aren't you?"

Anders nodded.

"*Oh*," said Rayna.

"Right," Sam agreed. "For the rest of you, there's a puppet show about the last great battle, and the players like setting up in Trellig Square. They have little Wolf Guard puppets, and little human puppets, and the dragon puppets . . . well, they breathe fire."

"How?" Isabina asked, immediately interested in how an invention like that would work.

"Jerro and I made a few coppers carrying supplies for them once, and one of the women told me," Sam said. "They said that kind of fire is made by using a special kind of salt and iron filings."

Everyone was listening now, his voice the only sound besides the crackling of the fire. "The salt turns the flame white, and the iron filings make it spit sparks."

Mikkel's mouth fell open. "You're saying it makes it look like dragonsfire."

"We were framed," Ellukka said, glancing around the circle as though somebody would be able to explain to her who had done this and why. "Someone lit those houses on fire and tried to pretend it was the dragons."

"You were framed," Sam agreed, "and we were almost killed."

"But who did it?" Rayna asked.

Anders had a horrible suspicion that he knew the answer to that, but it lurked in the corner of his mind, still half-hidden in the shadows. He had no proof, so at least for now, he said nothing.

* * *

It was hard to get to sleep that night with everybody staring at them, waiting for him and Rayna to pass out so they'd know whether Hayn's runes had worked or not.

Every time Anders moved, he felt the scratch of the paper against his chest where it was wrapped firmly around his augmenter, and every time he got settled, he found something else to poke him in the ribs or sit not quite right under his hip.

And then the next thing he knew, he was in Drifa's workshop.

Was he awake again? Had he been sleepwalking?

Rayna stood beside him, and when he reached out to catch her hand, his passed straight through it. She blinked, stared, and tried grabbing his hand, with the same result.

"Not awake, then," he concluded.

His voice caused a figure on the far side of the room to move, and Anders's attention snapped up as he realized they weren't alone.

It was a tall woman who, even in the dim light of the workshop, looked instantly like an older version of Rayna. Her skin was just the same shade, and her dark hair was tightly curled. It stood out in a ring around her head, as wide as it was tall. She wore a leather apron over her clothes, and it was pitted and scarred with little black scorch marks. It was a dragonsmith's apron.

"What are we doing here?" she asked, looking around the room, her gaze pausing on the two children.

Anders's tongue seemed to fill his mouth, but he made himself speak. "Are you Drifa?" he asked.

"Yes," she replied, coming around the table beside her to walk closer to the twins. "But who are you?"

"I'm . . . we're . . ." Anders could hardly make himself speak. "I'm Anders," he said, "and this is—"

"Rayna," his sister breathed.

"It can't be you," Drifa whispered. "It can't—you're both so big. Sparks and scales, has it really been so long?"

"It's been ten years," said Rayna quietly.

Drifa's lips trembled, and she pressed them together very hard, as though she was trying not to cry. "I've missed so much," she said quietly. "It's so, so good to see you both."

"Is our father here?" Rayna asked.

Drifa shook her head in a small, tight movement, but she took a long breath through her nose, and her voice was even when she replied, "No. Felix is gone."

"But you're not," Anders said quietly.

"Not yet," she corrected him gently.

"We can't get to you," he said. "We tried, and Cloud-haven led us to a wall covered in words. We're trying to translate them—a friend of ours, she knows how—but we haven't really gotten anywhere. If you can tell us what to do, we can come find you."

"No," Drifa said, gentle but firm. "No, please don't try. Please stay away. It's not safe."

Anders and Rayna exchanged a quick glance. Rayna's eyebrow flicked, and Anders inclined his head just a fraction. It was all they needed to say. *As if we're staying away,* and, *I know, but there's no need to tell her that right now.*

"I didn't know it had been so long," Drifa was saying. "Tell me about yourselves, my darlings. I want to know as much as I can."

And so they did, falling over themselves to share all the details of their lives, telling her about all the places they had found to live and to sleep, about the places where they had gotten their food, all the ways they had kept themselves safe and entertained themselves on the streets. They told her about the last great battle too, and she pressed one hand over her mouth in horror.

"I left you with a woman I knew," Drifa said eventually, slowly shaking her head. "She was a human, so I hoped you'd be safe until I could come back. I needed

90

to hide for a little—I was close to being found. But then I . . . couldn't. I couldn't come back. I wish I could have. I would have stood trial for something I didn't do, I would have taken the punishment, if I'd known it would have prevented so much death. My friend must have died in the battle, if you were found as orphans. I'm so sorry, my loves. I never meant for you to be alone."

"We had each other," Anders said, and Rayna reached out to try to squeeze his hand, though hers went right through it again.

"You were two years old," Drifa whispered. "I'm surprised you even remembered your own names. Your father helped choose them, you know."

"We knew our names," Rayna said. "And we knew we were twins. We stuck together."

The twins told Drifa about Kess the cat, about the friendly shopkeepers who had slipped them food. And they told her about the day they had found themselves down by the port, and had ended up on the dais, making their transformation, Rayna into a dragon and Anders into a wolf.

The story grew more somber as it went on, though. They told her about Rayna's time at Drekhelm and Anders's at Ulfar, about his journey to find her, about the smaller battle with their classmates, their time at the

Finskól, and the much larger battle for Holbard.

They told her how they had come to Cloudhaven now.

They told her they didn't know what to do next.

She listened to every word, drinking them up as if she were parched and their story was water. No detail was too small for her. Every triumph was to be celebrated. Every setback was met with sorrow. Anders had never had a more fascinated audience in his life.

"I think—" she began as they finished, then abruptly faded out of sight.

The twins had only time to gasp, and then she returned, translucent for a moment, then apparently solid once more.

"This is taking too much of my essence," she said. "I can't do it for much longer. Listen closely, my darlings. I'll answer as many of your questions as I can. To bring your friends inside Cloudhaven, all you need are yourselves and your augmenters. You're descended from me, and I am descended from . . . well, many generations of dragon-smiths, including one of the founders of Cloudhaven itself. Bring your friends to the entrance, one at a time. Place one hand on your augmenter and one on your friend, and introduce them to Cloudhaven. They'll be able to come inside after that."

"I don't suppose you know how to bring about peace

between wolves, dragons, and humans?" Rayna asked with a sigh.

"I'm afraid I'm no expert on peace," Drifa said sadly. "Felix and I wanted it very badly, though. That was one of the reasons we made a workshop here at Cloudhaven—so we could work toward peace in secret. You said you had my map? Most of the artifacts it leads to were items we made, or ancient items we restored, each of them one we hoped might help us find a way to create peace between the elementals of Vallen. Some of the artifacts were tools, some were weapons, but we never found a way to use them. And, of course, very few elementals agreed with what we were trying to do.

"Your last great battle might have been fought after I . . . left, but though we wanted peace, Felix and I were a part of starting that war. It was his death and my disappearance that helped destroy the last of the trust between the wolves and the dragons. But your father and I always saw the good in both the wolves and the dragons, and others can too."

"We do," Anders said. "We have friends who are wolves *and* dragons *and* humans."

"Then you have even more friends than we did," she said. "Speaking of friends, you should trust your uncle Hayn. He's a very good man. That's what your father would want as well. When you wake up, you'll find Felix's communicator just over there." She pointed at a towering stack of papers leaning against a small clockwork device. "It's part of a set of four. Hayn has one, and the other three are there. If they don't work at first, remember you can use your blood for more than proving your identity to an artifact. For an elemental as powerful as each of you, the essence in your blood can provide power to an artifact as well. Prick your finger, let the artifact have a drop of your blood, and I think you'll find it will work for a little longer, though eventually you'll want to take it to a dragonsmith for repairs."

"There's so much about the artifacts we don't know," said Anders desperately, and he knew a part of him really meant, *So please don't leave us. This is as good an excuse as any. Please stay and tell us about artifacts. Please stay and be our mother.*

"I know," said Drifa, a note of desperation in her voice. "Don't forget about my map. It will tell you where every one of my artifacts is to be found. Perhaps you'll know how to use them where I didn't. Be careful, though—it's not safe. There are those who will do anything to stop you."

She lifted her hand toward them, but she seemed to know without trying that it would pass straight through them, and so she didn't touch them.

As they watched, her hand faded out, then flickered back to life again.

"I love you," she said quietly. "I love you both more than anything. I'll try to come again if you need me."

"I . . . I love you too," Anders blurted out.

He had never said it to anyone except Rayna before.

"*We* love you," Rayna said.

And then the pair of them blinked awake, lying beside the fire.

For a long moment, Anders stared at the cracked ceiling, completely confused. Then he turned his head, and his eyes met Rayna's. As one, they scrambled to their feet. Most of their friends had fallen asleep waiting, but Ellukka and Sakarias were still awake, watching them for signs of life.

"Did it work?" Ellukka asked.

But Anders and Rayna were already running as fast as they could toward their mother's workshop.

When they stumbled through the door, they both pulled up short. Anders had known it would be empty—he had known she wouldn't be there—but he still felt in that moment like his heart might crack.

He made himself walk across the workshop to the pile of papers and the strange clockwork device. When he pushed them carefully to one side, there were three small communicator mirrors, just as she had said there would be. He flipped one open and stared down at the mirror, which showed him nothing except his own reflection.

Rayna silently unpinned her brooch, handing it across to him so he could prick his finger.

Soon, they would be able to speak to Hayn.

CHAPTER SIX

THE NEXT FEW DAYS RAN A LITTLE MORE smoothly. Anders and Rayna introduced their friends to Cloudhaven exactly as Drifa had told them to do, and then they tested whether it had worked with the same method they'd used to discover the twins could get inside in the first place.

Anders and Rayna watched from the hallway, and most of the others stood in the entrance hall, waiting nervously as Mateo and Bryn, two of the strongest of their number, held onto Theo's hands, as he was one of the lightest. If the floor crumbled beneath him when he stepped inside, as it had when they'd first arrived, they'd be ready to catch him and pull him up.

"Make sure you're holding on tight please," he said nervously, as he prepared to step backward onto the stone floor. "I don't have wings when I'm a human."

He reached back with one foot and rested it on a paving stone, waiting to see if it held. When it did, he slowly eased his weight onto it. Still it held.

"Here goes," he murmured, and moved his second foot back, so he was standing still on the stone floor. Then he let go of Mateo and Bryn's hands, and . . . nothing happened.

He was safely inside Cloudhaven.

Mikkel, Ellukka, and Sakarias danced in celebration, and Lisabet, Viktoria, and Isabina all watched with quieter satisfaction. Det nodded, as if he approved of Cloudhaven's decision.

Anders and Rayna both hugged Theo, who held on a little tightly, as if he still wasn't sure he was on firm ground. Bryn and Mateo just shook hands, then shook hands again, as if they were congratulating each other on their role.

"At last, proper beds," said Ferdie, grinning broadly.

"A proper kitchen," said Jai.

"More than one washroom," said Jerro.

Then Bryn and Mateo reached for Sam's hands, and prepared to hold him in place as Anders and Rayna made their next introduction to Cloudhaven. One by one the children were brought in, and with each new addition, Anders felt the hope inside him swelling. It felt good to achieve what they had set out to do.

Everyone immediately spread out to explore. Isabina headed for the mechanical room without delay, carrying a pile of books and promising they'd have running water and other helpful things in no time.

"Not," she said diplomatically, "that your drawing wasn't very useful, Rayna. I'm sure it gave me a head start on figuring out how it works."

That turned out to be a little optimistic, though, and some time later Anders found her sitting with Mateo, Theo, and Sam at the entrance to the strange room. It might have been where Cloudhaven had led them when they asked how to make it easier to stay there, but to him, it still looked more dangerous than anything else.

"We're getting there," Isabina promised. "Some of these instruments remind me of the ones at Drekhelm—I think they're artifacts that control the hot water and the lights and all kinds of things. But they were all designed so long ago that it's like trying to remember something you dreamed. Nothing's quite the same. We can figure it out together, though."

"She's right," Theo agreed. "Mateo thinks that section over there looks like something from Ulfar, so I'm about to squeeze in and go and poke at it."

"It's safer than it sounds," Sam promised, when he saw

Anders's face. "Once when I was, uh, passing through a fancy house in Holbard, I saw some gears just like this. I think it's fine if he touches them."

"Add in these books from Ulfar, and we're nearly there," Isabina promised. "Wolf, dragon, and human expertise, at your service."

Anders couldn't help smiling as he walked away. Of everyone, Isabina was perhaps the least concerned with the old enmity between wolves and dragons. She just wanted to invent things, and she didn't care who she did it with, as long as they were interesting.

One of the children's greatest concerns about Cloudhaven had been the fact that—just like its name suggested—it was permanently hidden in the clouds. That made it very hard to know if dragons were approaching. A few hours later, when Isabina and her team were able to switch on a series of alarms that would warn them if they had unexpected visitors, everyone breathed a sigh of relief. When they announced they'd managed running water as well—"And *hot* water!" Theo said, with a dragon's love of all things warm—their friends cheered out loud.

Meanwhile, behind the many doors of Cloudhaven, Anders and the others found lots of useful things, including bedrooms, and everybody moved inside to more comfortable surroundings. They also found empty forges, abandoned inventions, a banquet hall that would have seated at least a hundred people, and dozens of other strange rooms besides.

The big entrance hall remained the heart of Cloudhaven, though. There was always a fire burning in the fireplace, always at least a few children gathered around it to work or to talk.

They were in touch with Hayn every day via the communicator, and he reported that the camp outside Holbard continued to grow. He'd been on several scouting trips to the wolf camp to the north, though he couldn't go too close for fear he'd be seen and imprisoned again.

"I'd hoped to speak to them," he said via the mirror one night. "But the camp is set up for combat. I don't think they're in the mood to do anything but imprison me again, so I've kept my distance. They're training hard, every wolf down to the very youngest student. There's a fight coming, I'm sure of it."

In the meantime, the number of children they were sheltering at Cloudhaven continued to grow, filling up one bedroom after another. Hayn had a knack for finding those who had nobody else, and everyone at Cloudhaven knew that feeling far too well to deny them help—anything was better than the cold loneliness and the empty bellies that faced them in the camp.

They sourced their food sometimes from the camps, sometimes from Holbard, and sometimes they bought it from farms farther afield—the dragons were able to pose as travelers and spend their coins without suspicion.

But though they were busy rescuing children who needed them and making Cloudhaven into a home, Anders worried about the way the days were slipping away. They still had something much more important—and much harder—to achieve.

One evening he stood in the entrance hall, taking in the scene before him. Wolves, dragons, and humans were working together, cooking the evening meal, studying their stacks of books, or making the latest arrivals comfortable. They laughed and talked and squabbled, and though he knew not all of them had come around to trust those different from themselves, there was a kind of change in the air.

As Mateo and Bryn had said to him over lunch, it was hard to spend all day, every day, with someone, and hold on to your idea that they were all that different from you.

Anders finally felt as if they had stopped rushing from crisis to crisis, desperately trying to solve each one without time to think about how best to do it, and had earned themselves just a few moments of breathing space.

And though he never would have been able to admit it

out loud, he knew within himself that at least a little bit, he was responsible for what they had achieved so far. He was proud of that.

Still, the situation was definitely not without difficulties. Lisabet was subdued, and he knew that she was thinking about Sigrid, wondering what her mother's absence meant. There was a chance that Sigrid might be missing for the worst possible reason—that she'd been killed in the Battle of Holbard. But none of them really believed that. Someone, wolf or human, would have seen her fall, and everybody would be talking about the death of the Fyrstulf, the leader of the wolves.

It was far more likely that Sigrid was planning something, and Lisabet seemed to feel a kind of responsibility for her mother's actions that Anders wished she wouldn't. Lisabet wasn't the same as Sigrid—anyone who met her for even a minute knew that.

Bryn had succeeded in translating the glowing text on the wall that concealed Drifa, but that puzzle would not be as easy to solve as they had hoped. Some of the words made perfect sense. Others were in some kind of code.

"I can tell you what every one of these letters is," Bryn said with a sigh. "But if we're going to decode it, we need a key. Something that tells us what kind of code it really is. Until then, I don't know how we can get past the wall."

Despite his mother's warning not to come looking for her, Anders had spent a lot of time thinking about how they might reach her.

And through all these small triumphs and bigger challenges, one stood out as the hardest of all: they still had absolutely no idea how to convince the wolves, dragons, and humans outside of Cloudhaven that they needed to talk to one another if they were ever going to rebuild Vallen.

Later that night, Anders was returning from fetching more wood for the fire, along with Ellukka and Sam. Anders had asked Lisabet if she wanted to come, but she had quietly shaken her head and returned to the book she was reading. He wished he knew how to make her feel better.

The firewood came from a giant room not far inside Cloudhaven, where pieces of wood from kindling to logs had been neatly stacked by someone in the past. There was even a small red wagon on wheels for transporting the wood to whichever fireplace you were using, and just now Sam was towing it along, stacked high.

The three of them were walking in thoughtful silence through hallways that had quickly become familiar. These days, unless they were going somewhere new, they didn't even ask Cloudhaven to give them directions. They didn't need a glowing path to lead them to and from the fire-wood room.

It was Ellukka who suddenly stopped short and lifted one hand, causing Anders and Sam to halt as well. She had her head cocked to one side, as though she was listening for something, and Anders strained his ears but could hear nothing.

"Do you hear that?" Ellukka whispered, almost inaudible. "It sounded like a rock clacking against something."

Sam and Anders shook their heads, but then Anders suddenly remembered the sound that he had heard but never been able to explain. He pointed ahead of them and raised his eyebrows—*Was it that way?*—and she nodded.

The three of them began to creep carefully along the hallway, making as little sound as possible. The firewood cart had been as well-oiled as all the doors of Cloudhaven, and was silent as it trundled along behind Sam.

Last time Anders had heard the unexplained noise, he had called out. This time, they reached the corner in silence and carefully peeked around it all at once, Ellukka's head on top, Sam's at the bottom, and Anders's in the middle.

They stared for a long moment, then withdrew back around the corner to stare at each other with huge eyes.

They had all seen the same thing, but Anders could

tell from his friends' faces that they could barely believe it any more than he could.

What Anders had seen was . . . well, it looked like a huge person, at least seven feet tall, but it was made of clay, as best he could tell from this distance. It was obviously an artifact, not only because it was walking on its own, but also because it had a skeleton on the outside made from metal and teeming with runes.

They conducted a quick, completely silent conversation, raising their brows, widening their eyes, and gesturing wildly.

The language of wolves involved mostly body language—a tilt of the head or a flick of an ear was as good as a whole sentence. So even in human form, Anders suspected he understood the other two a little better than they understood him or each other. Ellukka wanted to go around the corner and confront the thing. Sam wanted to hide somewhere.

Anders, if he was completely honest with himself, wanted to hide somewhere as well. But he knew they couldn't. This place was so full of mysteries, they couldn't give up the chance to solve one. So he nodded to Ellukka, straightened his shoulders, and with Sam reluctantly behind them, they walked around the corner.

The giant artifact was walking slowly toward them,

and stopped in place as they came into sight. Well, possibly into sight. It didn't have eyes, so Anders had no idea if it could see them.

"What is it?" Sam whispered.

"Are you from Cloudhaven?" Anders asked it, raising his voice. "Are you what we've been hearing?"

It didn't answer, and it didn't move, simply gazing toward them.

Half a minute passed, and it was clear that nothing would happen unless the children made it. So Anders slowly walked up to the huge figure, tilting his head back to stare at it.

It responded then, bowing a little at the waist and tipping its head down to stare at him in return. Anders heard a series of clicks inside it, as though some cogs or gears were moving. Then it grabbed him tightly around the waist, lifting him clean off his feet. It tucked him under its arm and turned away from Ellukka and Sam, striding quickly down the hallway.

"Put me down!" Anders yelled, trying to push his way free, but the thing was made of rock, and he couldn't budge it an inch—it only tightened its grip uncomfortably around him and kept moving.

"Stop!" Ellukka screamed behind him. "Cloudhaven, stop it!"

But nothing happened.

Anders couldn't see behind the artifact, but he could hear Sam and Ellukka following, both shouting for it to stop as Anders continued the fight to kick and wriggle his way free. The artifact responded by picking up its pace until it was jogging, shaking Anders up and down in the process until he could barely keep his eyes open. His heart was racing now, the artifact's arm around him forcing him to take quick, shallow breaths.

His legs were sticking out behind it, and that was how he knew Ellukka—who so often used her strength to solve problems—had thrown herself at the creature. She wrapped her arms around the arm that held Anders, digging her heels into the ground, trying desperately to drag it to a stop, or at least slow it down.

Its step caught and it nearly stumbled, and for a moment it seemed as though she might succeed.

Then it shook itself impatiently, throwing her aside so she crashed into the rock wall.

"Now, Sam," she screamed from somewhere behind Anders. "Do it! Do it now!"

Anders wriggled and twisted again, and he caught a glimpse of Ellukka dragging herself to her feet, still dazed from the impact with the wall. With a few quick, stumbling steps, she ran ahead of the artifact warrior, but before Anders had time to understand or even really wonder what she was doing, something crashed into it from behind.

Sam had driven the firewood cart into the warrior's legs with all his strength, and it toppled backward, still holding tight to Anders, firewood scattering everywhere as they came to rest atop the cart.

Sam, his face grim with determination, kept pushing the cart as hard as he could, and his momentum carried him a little way despite its weight. Ahead, Ellukka had yanked open a door, and with one final shove, Sam pushed the cart, the artifact warrior, and Anders straight through the doorway, making a grab for Anders's hand as he did.

Anders locked one hand onto Sam's and grabbed at the doorframe with the other, trying desperately to free himself from the warrior so the others could slam the door. He could hear its internal gears clanking and grinding as it tried to climb out of the cart and back to its feet.

It moved its arm, and for one glorious moment, Anders was free of it.

Then its hand clamped down on his ankle with an iron grip, holding him so tight that Anders wondered for a terrifying moment if it was going to pull his foot off.

Ellukka was shouting something, ready to slam the

door closed, but he couldn't understand her. He gave one kick, and then another, and finally her words penetrated.

"Transform," she was screaming. "Change, Anders!"

In a flash, on instinct, he did as she said, throwing himself into his wolf form. And as he did, his leg became thinner and slipped free of the artifact warrior's grasp. He hurled himself out the door, landing on top of Sam, and Ellukka slammed it closed behind him, turning the lock with a loud click.

Without any need for consultation, all three of them turned to run back toward the entrance hall and the fire-place, Anders not even bothering to slip back into human form until they had stumbled out to the surprised group preparing for dinner.

Jai and Det lifted the cooking pot away from the flames, and all the others gathered around Anders, Ellukka, and Sam as they gasped out their story, adding details, trying to make sense of what had happened.

"We didn't ask Cloudhaven for directions," Anders said, still panting for breath, his heart refusing to slow down. "We knew the way to the firewood room. We didn't need them. Maybe that's why it didn't know we were there. There wasn't a path."

In the end, it was decided that they couldn't simply leave the artifact where it was. They banded together as a group, fifteen of them, wolves, dragons, and humans, making their way back inside, leaving some of the others to guard their newest arrivals.

They armed themselves as best they could with what they found in the rooms along the way, but when they reached the place where they had imprisoned the artifact, the door was still locked.

Ellukka opened it slowly and lifted her lamp, shining a light inside.

The room was completely empty, save for the broken red wagon and the scattered firewood. Apart from that it didn't contain a stick of furniture, not even a rug on the ground. There was no sign at all of where the warrior had gone.

A few of them stepped inside, shining their lamps around as though it might suddenly emerge from a crack in the walls, and they were about to leave again when Theo suddenly dropped to a crouch, brushing at the dust on the floor.

"Look here," he said, "these cracks, they're a square."

"He's right," said Mateo. "This is a trapdoor. This piece of rock, it should lift out somehow."

But try as they might, they couldn't work out how to budge it. It didn't have a ring sunk into it, and the crack around the edge was too narrow for even the smallest of them to get their fingers inside, so it was impossible to imagine the artifact warrior wedging its giant hands in. If this was where the warrior had gone, then it must have had some way to open the trapdoor that they couldn't understand.

"I have a question," said Mikkel as they puzzled over it. "Even if we could open this trapdoor, is that really what we want to do? I mean, if we're right, the warrior's down there. Are we sure we could win a fight against it?"

And the truth was, nobody was sure of that at all.

In the end, they locked the door again, retreated back to the fire, and made new rules. No one was to go inside Cloudhaven except in a large group. Nobody was to sleep in the bedrooms inside Cloudhaven. They would retrieve the mattresses and drag them out to lay them around the fire, sleeping in the entrance hall, as they had done at the beginning. They would make sure guards were always awake and on duty.

Nobody complained.

Soon Ferdie was singing as they set up the new camp, and Sakarias chased some of the smallest children around the fire, eliciting squeals of delight.

They all made the best of it, and Anders was so proud of them for that. But deep down, he felt they had taken yet another step back. This place had felt a little safer, like a base from which they could try to make everywhere else safer as well. And now it wasn't safe at all.

It made him ask himself if anywhere they went, if anything they did, would ever be enough. And he didn't know the answer to his own question.

CHAPTER SEVEN

THE NEXT DAY, ANDERS WAS ONE OF THE MEM-
bers of an expedition to the camp outside Holbard.

He was looking forward to it, in part because it would
be a chance to see Hayn in person rather than just speaking to him through the communicator mirror.

But he had another idea as well. Before he left, he
traded some of his clothes, swapping with the others until
he was dressed in the fanciest-looking outfit he could
manage. Rayna looked him up and down admiringly,
then snickered. "You look like someone rich," she teased
him. "Just goes to show, looks can be deceiving."

Lisabet was watching him, though, frowning faintly.
"You know what else he looks like," she said. "He looks a
little like a boy who was on a wanted poster just recently.
We've been keeping a low profile around the camp until
now, but dressed like that, you'll draw more attention. If

you're going to do that, you should take precautions." She went up on her toes and pulled Ferdie's knitted hat from his head, walking over to pull it on over Anders's curls. "That's a little better," she said. "The posters weren't up for long. You don't have to look that different."

Anders hoped she was right, and gave the hat an extra tug to pull it down a little farther as they prepared to take off.

Hayn had hiked out to the meadow to meet them where they usually landed—or, more likely, he had transformed into a wolf and enjoyed the run instead—and they all had a chance to talk to him as they made their way back in toward the camp. He slung an arm around Anders's shoulders and found something to say to each member of the group.

He reported that he was still coming and going, watching the wolves' camp from the outskirts without letting them see him, and spending some time at the human camp as well. Just as he concealed himself from the wolves, though, he also concealed himself from the humans—it was just that in their case, all he had to do was stay in his human form and make sure he wore nothing that looked like an Ulfar uniform.

When they reached the camp, Jerro, Theo, and a girl they'd rescued last trip, called Zil, peeled away to search the darker, muddier areas of the camp and see if there were any children who needed help.

Ferdie, who was visiting on medical duty, headed off with Sam, who had come to act as his assistant. Now that the camp facilities were slowly becoming more organized, Ferdie had to pretend that he was a doctor's assistant himself, because nobody would take someone his age seriously. But he was still able to do quite a lot, and particularly for the people in the camp who weren't willing to visit the medical tents, or weren't well enough to go.

"That just leaves us," Hayn said to Anders. "You look like you have a plan in mind. What do you want to do?"

Anders grinned—Hayn was learning to read his expression far more quickly than he'd have expected. But then again, their faces were so similar, perhaps it was simply like reading his own.

"I want to get a closer look at the mayor," he said. "If any of this is going to be fixed, if anything's going to change, then the mayor as the head of the humans, Professor Ennar as the head of the wolves, and Leif and the Dragonmeet will all have to be willing to talk to each other. And the mayor's the one I know least about. I have to figure out what he's like if I'm going to make it happen."

"We can certainly try," Hayn agreed. "The mayor isn't

likely to be interested in talking to you without a reason—you're a child, and he's a very busy man. I'm guessing that's where I come in."

"I'll have a better chance with you," Anders agreed.

"Well," said his uncle, "you're the one with a lifetime of clever plans behind you. Tell me what you have in mind."

Anders liked that that was the way Hayn thought of it—a lifetime of clever plans—when he could have so easily looked down on Anders. So many people had no time at all for the children of Holbard's streets, saw them only as pests to be chased away. But Hayn seemed to find something to admire in his and Rayna's survival.

Anders and his uncle took up a position near the front of the mayor's tent. It was easily the largest in the camp, the canvas walls sturdy, the guy ropes taut. Anders was fairly sure that it was the only place that remained dry when the rain swept through.

Just like the first day they visited, there were long lines of people snaking up to the tables that were set outside the tent, waiting their turn to make a request or lodge a complaint. The mayor had clearly given up on hearing them personally, and now the tables were manned by aides instead.

"There's always more people waiting to speak to

someone," Anders said quietly. "Have any of their requests been answered yet?"

"I don't think so," Hayn replied. "But the line is so long, nobody's made it to the front twice. So they can't exactly come back to complain about it, can they?"

Anders watched the harried clerk, who did at least seem to be listening to the woman at the front of the line and jotting down notes. The stack of papers beside him was growing perilously tall, and when a breeze blew through the camp, it swayed—he had to grab at it to stop it from toppling over into the mud.

It looked like Anders's idea was going to work. He pulled Hayn down so he could whisper in his uncle's ear, and after a short conference, Hayn strode confidently up to the clerk's desk.

"They sent me out to bring these inside," he said, reaching for the pile of papers. "Looks like I'm just in time."

The clerk turned his head to look up at Hayn, frowning for a moment, because, of course, he didn't recognize him. But Hayn simply shuffled the giant stack of papers into place and hefted it into his arms. Anders had told him, *Nine-tenths of it is acting like you're meant to be there*, and Hayn had clearly taken his advice to heart. After a long moment, the clerk simply nodded and added his current piece of paper to the stack.

"Please send someone out here to relieve me," he said plaintively. "Tell them I haven't had a break in hours."

Hayn promised he would and turned away, pausing to let Anders take some of the stack so they could each carry a pile of papers into the tent.

Beyond the flap there was a table surrounded by a mismatched collection of chairs, with a series of rugs on the ground to keep away the worst of the mud, and along one wall sat stack after stack of paperwork. It was clear that once the requests and complaints came inside this tent, nobody touched them.

Anders felt terrible for the people who had spent days lining up to lodge them, but as someone who had spent most of his life trying to get his hands on things he needed, he was also privately impressed that the mayor's aides had managed to find this much paper.

The mayor, who was a tall, skinny man with light-brown skin and thinning black hair, was running one hand over his bald spot, as if intent on removing the last of his hair.

His assistants were all keeping out of the way while he talked to a short, muscular woman with gray hair clipped close to her head. She had her back to them, and Hayn and Anders took up a position by the door, so as not to interrupt, or worse, be spotted and told to leave.

"I hope you're not expecting me to listen to you while you're using that tone of voice," the mayor was saying to the woman, running his hand agitatedly across his hair again.

Anders had watched the mayor stand silently next to Sigrid at the monthly Trial of the Staff for years—the man wasn't used to standing up for himself. The attention had always been on the Fyrstulf. She had been the one who gave the speeches. She had been the one who commanded the ceremony. The wolves had run things in Holbard all Anders's life. But it sounded like the mayor was finally using some of his authority.

"Your people threw *rocks*!" the woman snapped, and both Anders and his uncle froze in place at the sound of her voice.

That wasn't just any woman. That was Professor Ennar. She wasn't wearing her Ulfar uniform, but there was no mistaking her. She was Hayn's friend, and had been Anders's combat teacher. She was a famous wolf warrior—during the last great battle, she and her wife had defended a whole section of the city wall by themselves for a full hour. The wolves still told the story ten years later. She'd led Anders's class on a rescue mission to Drekhelm when she'd thought he and Lisabet were in danger. She was fierce and big-hearted, but she was still a wolf, which meant she'd still see both of them as traitors.

Anders spun around and pretended to busy himself tidying the stacks of paper along the back wall of the tent, head down, and after a second Hayn caught on and joined him.

"I can't be responsible for what every one of my people does," the mayor replied firmly. "You've just been telling me you can't be held responsible for the wolves who started the battle, so I'm sure you understand my point of view."

"I *understand* that what's happening is unacceptable," Ennar replied, with a growl in her voice. "I have students with me at our camp, they're just children. And they have human families, you know."

"Unacceptable? Who are you to decide that? Where's your leader?" the mayor demanded. "Where's Sigrid?"

"That's wolf business," Ennar snapped. Anders glanced sideways at Hayn, who grimaced. Anders was sure that Ennar was avoiding answering because she didn't know where Sigrid was.

"If you want us to trust you, then—"

"*Trust* us?" Ennar growled. "You should *thank* us!"

"For destroying the city?"

"For saving as many people as we did!"

"Listen," said the mayor, managing a hint of a growl himself. "The dragons weren't attacking us. They were attacking *you*. When we rebuild Holbard, it'll be a city for humans. If there aren't any wolves within our walls, the dragons will leave us alone."

"You wouldn't dare," Ennar breathed. "You've lost your minds if you think you can protect yourselves. And where do you suggest we go? Holbard is our home!"

"Holbard *was* your home," the mayor corrected her. "It's not there anymore, because you and the dragons destroyed it."

Ennar didn't reply, but a moment later Anders heard her footsteps as she stalked past him, and then the tent flaps fell back into place behind her.

Slowly, carefully, Anders and Hayn turned to face the mayor. He was still studying the way Ennar had gone, but then his gaze shifted across to Hayn, and he blinked.

"I didn't see you come in," he said, making a visible effort to pull himself together, standing up a little straighter. He sighed softly and sank down into his chair. "You can't be serious. You haven't brought more requests?"

"I'm afraid so, sir," said Hayn. "The line outside is still very long. And your clerk is asking for someone else to come take a turn hearing the complaints."

"Don't they know we don't have any power to help

them?" the mayor demanded. "There's not a secret stock-pile of food in here. What could we possibly give them?" There was a kind of desperation to his tone, and he looked at Hayn as if he really might answer him.

Anders looked around at the unpatched walls of the tent, at the rugs on the floor, at the furniture, at the remains of the meal he could see on the table. If the mayor thought this was hardship, what would he think of the worst parts of the camp? Did he even know what was happening out there?

"Herro Mayor," Anders began, before he even knew that he meant to speak to the man. He'd only intended to learn more about him, but now he found that wasn't enough.

The mayor blinked and leaned sideways to see better around Hayn, studying Anders as though he had only just realized he was there. "Who is this child?" he asked, in the same voice that some people would say, *What is this insect?*

"My assistant," said Hayn.

Anders had a lot of experience sensing when he was about to be thrown out of somewhere, and he could hear it in the mayor's voice now. He knew exactly what Rayna would do, and quickly, he tried it.

"I'm sorry," he said in his most respectful voice. "I

don't mean to interrupt, Herro Mayor. I know you're doing something very important. But there are lots of rumors out there. People are wondering about the wolves. We could answer their questions without them ever coming inside to you if we knew a little more."

The mayor seemed somewhat mollified by this show of respect, and also interested in the idea of being left alone by everyone.

"We're finished putting up with the wolves," he replied. "It was their explosion of cold that nearly destroyed the city, and they failed to protect us when we needed them most. After a decade of promising us that they would defend us when the next great battle came, they left Holbard in ruins. The wolves have been grabbing for power for far too long, and whatever game they were playing this time, it went too far."

Anders couldn't help wondering if the wolves' grab for power had gone even further than the mayor knew. There was the fake dragonsfire to think of, after all, and the Wolf Guard had been seen more and more around Holbard in recent months. The very day of Anders and Rayna's transformations, the twins had been dodging guards all the way down to the port. The wolves had been everywhere, frustrating Holbard's citizens, and all on the basis of a couple of dragon sightings.

Perhaps the mayor was right in part, and the wolves had been reaching for power—he could tell the mayor certainly saw this as his chance to get his power back.

Anders didn't know what his face was doing as these realizations came to him, but the mayor clearly read his expression as meaning he was worried.

"Come here," he said, a little bit gentler. "Everything will be all right. I'm going to look after our people."

For a moment, Anders could see why the mayor had been voted in. When he remembered to smile, he was charming.

That didn't change what Anders thought of how the mayor was distributing resources at the camp, though. It didn't change the fact that he was in a comfortable tent, while there were families and children out in the cold.

"Are people really talking about this?" the mayor asked. "Are they worried about the wolves?"

"People are scared," Anders told him, "and they aren't seeing you. They don't know what you're doing to protect them."

The mayor considered this, and then he nodded slowly. "Young man," he said, "you're right. This afternoon, I'm going to walk through the camp. See people. Talk to them."

"Herro Mayor," protested one of his aides, "we can't

possibly provide you with security."

The mayor waved a hand at him. "If I need security in my own camp, then the problem is bigger than I thought," he said. "It's important. I want to see the camp. All of it."

He was already turning back to the aides, and Hayn rested his hand on Anders's shoulder. "We should go. Thank you for your time, Herro Mayor."

"No," said the mayor, "thank you for taking the time to talk to me. I need to hear from more people."

As Anders and Hayn beat their retreat, Anders tried to make sense of what had just happened. Nothing the mayor was doing seemed best for the camp, but the man had just taken the time to explain things to Anders, to listen to him, and even to take his advice. It didn't much change Anders's opinion of him, but it was a reminder that, like the wolves, and like the dragons, the mayor was more complicated than Anders had assumed.

But, said a voice in his head, *he only listened to you because he had absolutely no idea who you were. If he'd known you were a wolf like Ennar, or if he'd thought you were a street orphan, he'd have thrown you out in an instant.*

"At least you made a little progress," said Hayn.

"You know," said Anders slowly, as a thought came to him, "I think we just made a lot of progress. I think I know what we have to do."

"And what's that?" asked Hayn.

"He listened to us," said Anders, "because he didn't know who we were. He listened to our ideas and our thoughts because he thought that we were like him, instead of being different. That was why I borrowed everyone's best clothes today. I thought it might help me get in, but it did even more than that. We have to find a way to get them all to talk to each other without knowing who the other ones are."

Hayn frowned, thoughtful. "I see what you're saying. But how can you disguise the identities of so many people?"

"I have no idea," Anders admitted. "But I know there's going to be a way. All we have to do is find it. There's an artifact for everything, Hayn."

"True," his uncle agreed. "There might be something in the books you salvaged from Holbard. But if you can speak to your mother again, that's what you should do. She knew more about the artifacts all around Vallen than anyone I've ever met. She might even have an artifact of her own that you can find using her map."

"She did tell me the map led to all her artifacts," Anders said thoughtfully. "We just have to know which one to ask it for."

"Then that's what you should do," Hayn said. He

hesitated, and then continued. "And will you tell her . . . tell her I'm sorry, Anders. I didn't know she and my brother were in love, and I wish they'd told me. I'd have tried to protect them. I can't help wondering if they thought I'd object like everyone else did. Tell her I'm going to watch out for you and Rayna. That you still have a family."

Anders swallowed hard against the lump in his throat, but he nodded, and Hayn squeezed his hand.

Soon it was time for the two of them to part ways, and Anders pulled his cloak tight around himself against the bitter wind as he walked out to their landing place with Ferdie and Sam to meet Jerro, Zil, Theo, and whoever they had found that day.

But despite the cold, there was something warm inside him, and it wasn't just because of the message Hayn had asked him to give his mother.

He didn't know how to pull it off yet, but he knew he had the beginnings of a plan.

CHAPTER EIGHT

ANDERS WAS STILL THINKING ABOUT HIS PLAN that evening, but as night drew around them, he had to admit he was also thinking a lot about dinner.

Jai and their assistants were cooking up a big meal to welcome the newest arrivals—there were now nearly fifty children at Cloudhaven, with beds set up all over the entrance hall. It was a little crowded, but it was still a hundred times better than the cold, wet, and muddy camp, where they had nothing to shelter under except thin blankets—and some didn't even have those, the orphans of Holbard pushed to the very outskirts of the camp.

Here, the fire was big and warm, and they had draped a large piece of canvas across the archway that led to the landing pad, which kept most of the wind out. They'd dragged mattresses from the bedrooms, so they had somewhere to sleep, and there was enough to eat. ("And if that scary artifact warrior tries to chase me while I'm having a hot shower," Sam had said, when they got the bathing chambers working, "then it's just going to have to wait until I'm done.")

It had been a long day at the camp, and Anders was glad to be home. He was still stretching out his muscles from the flight, and was on his way over to see whether he could help Jai and the other cooks when the door to Cloudhaven proper flew open with a bang.

Bryn came running out, followed by Isabina, Viktoria, Jerro, Det, and, finally, Sakarias—following the rules, they had gone in as a group so that Bryn could check a couple of the letters in the message on Drifa's wall that she was still trying to decode.

Now, her eyes were wide, hair streaming out behind her as she ran. "Warrior!" she screamed.

And then it was through the door behind them.

The hall exploded into chaos as the children scattered to make way for the creature, and despite its huge, lumbering form, it was surprisingly quick as it pounded after Sakarias, the nearest of its quarry.

The others peeled off to the edges, but Sakarias couldn't shake it. Anders caught a glimpse of his pale face as he bolted past, heading for the door that led out to the landing pad. When he burst through it, the artifact warrior rumbled straight through after him.

Most of the children ran to hide in the shadows, but the elementals, Sam, and Jerro hurtled out onto the landing pad after them, desperate to somehow help Sakarias.

He had backed up nearly to the edge now, and the warrior was advancing on him with a slow, purposeful step.

Jai hurled an empty cooking pot at it, and caught the warrior square between the shoulder blades, but the pot simply bounced off it and clanged away into the misty night.

Without thinking, Anders and the other former Ulfar students slipped into their wolf forms, growling low in their throats as they crept forward toward the warrior. There was a rush of wind behind him, and when he turned his head, he saw that Ellukka had thrown herself into dragon form. But she had the same problem they did. The warrior was so close to Sakarias now that anything they did to attack it, knock it over, or even push it over the edge, was liable to hit Sakarias as well.

Sakarias took another step backward and his heel reached the edge of the cliff, tiny pieces of rubble falling away into the silent clouds all around him.

Then it all happened at once. The warrior flung its arms out and lunged forward for Sakarias. Nimble, he twisted and ducked, and almost made it under the warrior's arm, *almost* made it to safety.

But its fingers hooked into the edge of his cloak, and as it tumbled off over the edge of the cliff, Sakarias only had time for a startled scream before he was yanked with it.

Viktoria's howl split the air.

And then Ferdie, still in human form, was running past Anders, legs pumping, accelerating toward the edge.

He threw himself off the cliff, arms spreading out as though they were wings—but they weren't, and had no chance of slowing him—and then he vanished into the fog.

The pack ran to the edge of the cliff, staring desperately over it. But Cloudhaven still lived up to its name, and the warrior, Sakarias, and Ferdie had all completely disappeared into the mist.

They stood there, hearts hammering in their chests, and one by one, returned to human form, still standing in a line, staring at where their friends had disappeared. Viktoria was sobbing, and Anders couldn't make himself move, or speak, or believe what he had just seen.

And then the mist parted, and a dragon became visible, winging his way back up toward Cloudhaven.

Ferdie had Sakarias clutched in his claws, and Sakarias had both arms wrapped around Ferdie's leg. The wind buffeted the children waiting for them as Ferdie hovered, carefully depositing Sakarias on the ground, then landing himself so he could slip back into human form.

Viktoria pushed past the others, running straight for Sakarias to throw her arms around him and began instantly to berate him.

"What were you thinking?" she demanded. "How did you let it get so close to you? What were you doing near the edge? Why don't you ever think, Sak? Why don't you ever . . ." Her words ran out, and she buried her face against his shoulder as Sakarias carefully wrapped his arms around her.

"Are you okay?" Anders asked carefully.

Sakarias opened his mouth to reply, but Viktoria beat him to it.

"Of course he's okay," she replied. "Can't you see I'm conducting a medical exam?"

Sakarias didn't look too unhappy about it, and he kept one arm around Viktoria as he looked across at Ferdie, whose always-laughing face was grave. "Thank you, Ferdie," he said quietly.

"We're friends," Ferdie said simply. "We have to stick together."

Sakarias, who Anders knew hadn't always felt the same way about Ferdie, simply nodded. Whatever he had thought in the past, his direct gaze said that now, Ferdie was right. They were friends. And they would stick together.

"For now," said Ferdie, "I have my own very important medical test to conduct to see whether Sakarias really is all right."

Sakarias's eyes went wide, and he glanced down at himself, as though there might be some damage he hadn't yet discovered.

"Sak," said Ferdie seriously, "are you hungry?"

"I could eat," Sakarias admitted as the others burst into laughter around him.

"He'll be fine," was Ferdie's prognosis.

Slowly, they all began to trickle back inside.

Anders heard Ellukka speak as she fell into step with Ferdie behind him. "How did you know you were going to transform before you hit the ground?" she said. "It must have been incredibly close."

There was a long silence, and Anders strained his ears as he waited for Ferdie's reply.

"I didn't," admitted Ferdie. "But things are pretty bad, Ellukka, and we're the only ones with a chance of changing that. We all have to be prepared to do whatever we can. We *have* to stick together."

As Anders stepped inside with the others, ready to try to explain what had happened, ready to try to make a new plan, he knew that Ferdie was right.

Whatever it took, he would do it.

But the more he thought about it, the more he realized that the warrior had changed things. It was all very well for the elementals to stay here at Cloudhaven despite the danger. With the humans and wolves hostile to them after the destruction of Holbard, this place was still safer than the town camp, and a better place to search for an answer.

But that wasn't true for everyone at Cloudhaven.

His heart was heavy as he made his way over to where Sam and Jerro were sitting with a group of other humans, talking quietly. They all looked up as Anders arrived, taking in his expression.

"He figured it out," Sam said to his big brother, who nodded.

"Looks like he's going to say it now," he said.

"Say what?" Anders asked.

Sam snorted. "You're about to tell us that it would be safer for us if we went back to the camp. That you could give us supplies, and we could be somewhere where there aren't giant artifact warriors trying to chase us off cliffs."

Anders blinked. "Well, um . . ." He hadn't expected them to anticipate his words. "You *could* go back to the camp. Where there really *aren't* giant artifact warriors trying to chase anyone off cliffs."

He realized he was speaking into silence—the wolves and the dragons around them were listening for the humans' reply.

Sam and Jerro exchanged a long look. "We humans already talked it over," said Sam. "We discussed it before tonight. We knew something like this might happen. And we decided that you were there for us when we needed you. And now we're here for you. However we can help, we're going to do it. We're staying."

"All of us," Jerro added. And behind them, the other children murmured their agreement, a few folding their arms, as if they were daring Anders to throw them out of Cloudhaven.

But he didn't know what to say. He remembered the way he'd heard the wolves use the word *human* when he first arrived at Ulfar Academy. Like a human was something less than an elemental. But the humans had a bravery and ingenuity that any elemental would be proud of. *Human* was a badge of honor.

"Then I guess we're all staying," he said, a lump in his throat. "We'll figure this out together."

* * *

Anders found it hard to get to sleep that night after the scare the warrior had given them, and he lay on his mattress, listening to the slow breathing of the others, gazing up at the dimly lit ceiling of the entrance hall. He and Rayna had carefully wrapped their augmenters in the rune-covered paper that would, they hoped, summon their mother.

One moment he was counting cracks in the rock, and the next moment he was in his mother's workshop once more.

Rayna was already waiting, and she turned to him with a grin.

"I thought you were never going to fall asleep," she said. "She's not here yet. I'm hoping she was just waiting for two of us."

And as if to prove Rayna's words true, Drifa appeared in front of them.

She didn't look the same as she had last time, though. Now, she was semi-transparent—if Anders concentrated, he could make out the bench that was behind her.

"It's so good to see you, my darlings," she said. "Has it been long?"

"Not long at all," Anders replied. "Are you all right?"

"We don't have much time," she said. "Tell me how I can help you."

As quickly as he could, Anders recounted what he had realized that day at the camp with Hayn.

"He's right," Rayna agreed. "We need to find a way to make them listen to each other's words, rather than thinking about who's speaking."

Drifa's mouth was open. "You *are* right," she breathed. "We never saw that. We were always looking for ways to stop them fighting, to make them afraid to fight or unwilling to fight. But it's more than that, isn't it?"

Anders nodded. "They need to understand each other," he agreed, "and they need to understand the humans too—and respect them. They *all* need to really listen, instead of blocking their ears because it's their enemy talking."

Drifa smiled slowly. "So if they really can't see who's talking, all they *can* do is listen," she murmured. "Look at you two, my children. You have dragon blood and wolf blood, and you were raised among humans. Of *course* you see all the sides of the story. We never did."

"Are there artifacts that can help?" Anders asked, hope welling up inside him.

Drifa nodded. "There are two. The first is the Mirror of Hekla. It's hundreds of years old. Felix and I restored it together—as dozens of designers and dragonsmiths must have done before us. The second is the Staff of Reya, which we made together. You've seen magical mirrors and staffs before—you have communicator mirrors, and I'm sure the wolves still use the Staff of Hadda for their monthly transformation trials. It was part of what inspired us to create the Staff of Reya, but I never thought of using it with the Mirror of Hekla before."

"We need both?" Anders asked.

"I'm sure you will," she replied. "I've seen the wolves and dragons try to talk before. You can find both artifacts using my map. If you found the Sun Scepter, you'll find the mirror and staff easily. I didn't hide the artifacts I hoped would bring peace nearly as carefully as I hid the weapons."

"But you never got the chance to use them," Rayna said quietly.

"No," said Drifa sadly. "We . . . no, we didn't. And now they've been left alone for more than a decade, so they'll need to be repaired. Take them to the dragonsmiths Tilda and Kaleb. When you were babies, they had an aerie in the hermits' caves. I doubt they've moved. You'll need Hayn as well."

A flash of memory hit Anders—he'd seen those names

before. Tilda and Kaleb were listed in the Skraboks, the huge books back at Ulfar that had listed the designers and dragonsmiths of all the greatest artifacts in Vallen. There had been entries for Drifa, Felix, and Hayn as well.

"Can't you just tell us where these artifacts are?" Rayna asked.

Drifa laughed. "Darlings, when I knew the truce was coming to an end, I hid dozens of artifacts we'd made and repaired—more than a hundred. I don't remember where each one was, but the map will show you."

No sooner was she finished speaking than she faded out of sight. Anders gasped, and felt a rush of relief as she slowly appeared once more.

"Hayn wanted me to give you a message," he said hurriedly. "He said to tell you that he would have tried to protect you and Felix, if he'd known. And that he'll be our family now."

Drifa pressed a hand to her heart, closing her eyes for a moment. "I wish we'd told him," she murmured. "He deserved our trust. We would have, in time."

"I'll tell him that," Anders promised.

She nodded. "I'm afraid I won't be back again, my darlings. I don't have enough essence left in me. Too much is gone."

"No," Rayna murmured, starting forward, then remembering they couldn't touch. "Tell us where you are, we can find you!"

"No," said Drifa firmly. "It's not safe. I told you there were those who didn't agree with your father and me, who didn't want peace. I don't want to put you in their path if I can help it."

"But we need more time," Anders protested. "We only just met you."

"It breaks my heart to go," Drifa said, tears in her eyes. "I wanted to do . . . well, everything. But I'm so grateful we got to meet. Please tell Hayn I'm trusting him to take care of you. And I know how strong you both are. I'm trusting you to take care of each other, and love each other as much as I love you."

And then, reaching one hand out, as though she wanted to touch them, she faded from sight once more.

This time, she did not reappear.

When Anders woke, his eyes were wet with tears, and Rayna was sniffling softly, crawling onto his mattress to creep under his blanket and curl up against him. He felt a series of needles sink into his leg as Kess climbed up his body as well, finding a place between the two of them.

It seemed so desperately unfair, to be without their

mother all their lives, to find her, and then to lose her so soon afterward. Anders had wondered who his parents were growing up, but he had never felt the pain of their absence like he did now. Now he could imagine what it would have been like to have Drifa and Felix in his life.

He didn't sleep again, but instead lay where he was and waited for the dawn.

CHAPTER NINE

THE NEXT MORNING, ANDERS WAS TIRED—BUT more than that, he felt exhausted inside, as though his heart was tired too.

As he shuffled along the queue for breakfast, Lisabet fell into step with him. He took a sidelong look at her as Det spooned porridge into their bowls. After the events of last night, he felt like he understood a little more of what Lisabet was going through than he had before. Without a word, he linked his arm through hers and led her outside.

They made their way across the landing pad, although they stopped some distance short of the edge, still thinking of Sakarias's fall the day before. As they settled down and dug their spoons in, she gave him an expectant look. "What is it?" she asked.

"I wanted to talk," he replied. "Or more, I wanted to listen."

"To me?"

He nodded, and she scooped up another spoonful of porridge, blowing on it to cool it down, and swallowing it before she spoke. "Has something happened, Anders? You look a little like someone chewed you up and spat you out."

He hesitated, but Lisabet had been so subdued lately, and he wanted so badly to show her he cared about her worries. If he was asking her to share them, perhaps he should go first, to show her how much he trusted her.

He told her what Drifa had said, and not just about the artifacts. He told her that his mother was gone now, and about the emptiness he felt.

"And you must have been feeling this way ever since the battle at Holbard," he said quietly. "Your mother's missing, it must be so hard."

Lisabet gave a sigh. "It is," she admitted. "And it's complicated too. Yes, I'm worried about her and scared for her, but I'm also angry at what I'm pretty sure she's done."

"We don't know that Sigrid did anything," he tried, but the protest sounded weak, even to him.

"We don't *know*," Lisabet conceded, "but I think she lit those fake fires in Holbard."

Anders's heart sank. "But when we were at Drekhelm, we found a map with the place the fire was lit marked on it," he pointed out.

"I know," she agreed, "and at the time, I suspected the dragons of lighting the fires. But now we know they're fake, I just don't see it anymore. I think, if anything, the dragons were investigating who lit the fires, because they knew they *didn't* light them. Can you imagine the Dragonmeet managing to agree on a plan as complicated as creating fake dragonsfire, when they know how to light real fires? They spend all day debating what to have for breakfast, Anders."

"I know," he agreed. "I just . . . I don't see why she would do something like that."

"I do," Lisabet replied with a sigh. "I mean, you told me what the mayor said to you yesterday, and he was right. She does basically want to rule Holbard—all of Vallen if she could. Do you remember the time we both snuck inside her office? You were trying to find out about Fylkir's chalice, and we ended up locked inside?"

"I remember," he said, and they both smiled, despite the seriousness and the sadness of the moment. They'd been hiding behind opposite couches, and when their eyes had met, their friendship had really begun.

"Well, she and Ennar were talking then," Lisabet said, "and my mother was saying that the humans couldn't be trusted to make their own decisions, that it was up to us to do what we had to do to keep them safe. Now I think we know what she believed she had to do. She had to scare them enough that they'd let her be in charge, and in the end, she might even have *wanted* a battle, if she thought she could win it. I wish it was different, and I miss her, and I don't know if she's safe, wherever she is. But I have to do what *I* believe in as well. And that means finding a way to get the wolves, the dragons, and the humans to listen to each other. Somehow."

They were both silent for a long moment, and then she offered him a small smile—and though it was weak, it was real. "Thank you for listening," she said softly. "Sometimes that's what I need most of all."

After breakfast, Anders, Rayna, Lisabet, Ellukka, Mikkel, and Theo gathered around Drifa's map. They were the six who had used the map to hunt for the pieces of the Sun Scepter together.

"This is just like old times," Rayna said as she smoothed the map out on the stone and pricked her finger. "We've already solved four riddles. We can manage two more."

She carefully squeezed a drop of blood onto the compass rose.

"We want to find the Mirror of Hekla," she told it clearly.

The map itself was a beautiful thing, made of cloth woven through with silvery thread that Drifa had somehow forged straight into the fabric. Every artifact was made by both wolves and dragons—the wolves designed the artifacts and created the right combination of runes to tell them what to do, and the dragons forged them in their essence-infused dragonsfire. Drifa had been a dragonsmith, and Felix and Hayn designers. For the first time, Anders wondered if his father had been the one to design the runes that must be engraved onto the silver thread, so small they couldn't be seen.

As he watched, the intricate knotwork around the map's edges started to wriggle, changing and rearranging itself until it spelled out letters instead of its closely woven pattern.

"Three blue buttons, one by one.
Only the smallest permits the sun.
Look southwest and you will see
It's guarded by a single tree."

Six heads bent over the map, and they studied it together in silence.

"I wonder if it means the southwest of all Vallen or if we figure out the area where it's hidden, and it's in the southwest part of *that*," Theo mused.

"Vallen," said Lisabet confidently, pointing to the lower left-hand side of the map. "Look here. The Brengun Lakes."

Anders squinted at where she was pointing. There was a river running from north to south, and three times it swelled out into a lake, then narrowed again. In the center of each of the three lakes was an island, and sure enough, they looked like three buttons on a shirt, one above the other.

"The top one looks smallest," Rayna said, "though sometimes the map isn't that accurate. I wonder what it means by 'permits the sun.'"

"Well," said Anders, "let's find out. It's not far away."

Mikkel nodded. "You go," he said, his voice teasing. "Theo and I are used to handling everything else."

Anders shot him a quick grin, remembering the pair's elaborate efforts to fool the Dragonmeet into thinking their friends were still somewhere at Drekhelm. "You can eat our dinner if we're back late," he promised.

They packed up some food, found the girls' harnesses, and launched from the landing pad, leaving behind their

148

friends as they turned southwest.

When they cleared the fog around Cloudhaven, it turned out to be a bright, sunny day, though it was cold so high up. They left the Icespire Mountains behind them and crossed the Efrivain River, which tumbled along beneath, young and lively at its source up in the mountains.

They kept to the north of the village of Little Dalven, and soon after that, they saw a new river beginning up in the highlands.

At first, it was just hints of white water and glints in the sun, hidden in among the rocks. But soon it gathered momentum, and as Rayna tilted her wings to allow Anders a better look at the ground, he saw it snaking down south toward the sea, tumbling through the golden green of the grass on its way to Port Baernor.

Just as the map had promised, three times it swelled out to make a lake, and each of the three lakes bore an island. The lower two were covered in trees, but the highest and smallest was covered in grass, marked only by a single tree that had grown taller than the highest building in Holbard, stretching its limbs up joyfully toward the sun.

Anders considered the shade of the two larger islands. That confirmed it. This was the only island that permitted the sun to touch it.

Rayna and Ellukka obviously agreed, for after a short, trumpeted exchange, the girls began to spiral down, landing side by side on the smallest of the three islands. Anders slid down his sister's shoulder and tugged free her harness, so she could transform without becoming tangled in it.

"This is the place," she said as soon as she was back in human form.

"And that's the tree," Anders agreed. "It's the only landmark on the island. Let's start by digging around its roots and see if Drifa buried the mirror there."

It turned out that the artifact was only half a foot beneath the surface, wrapped up in a waterproof cloth to keep the dirt away from it. Drifa had been right—the weapons had been harder to find than the artifacts meant for peace.

Lisabet carefully lifted it out of the hole and peeled the cloth aside, revealing a small, round mirror about the size of a dinner plate, with an intricately carved pattern of runes all around the edges. Some of them looked worn, and the mirror itself was dull, but all four of them leaned over it anyway, squinting at their blurry reflections.

"I wonder what it actually does," Anders said as he lifted his head once more. "It . . ." But he trailed away, because he had his answer. Seated around the mirror, and staring at him with amazed expressions, were three other versions of himself.

"You all look like me," said one of them in his voice.

"No, you all look like *me*," insisted another.

"You definitely . . . oh," said the third.

"I'm Anders," tried Anders, "and I'm seeing three of me."

"I'm Rayna," said one of the other Anderses, "and I'm telling you, there are three Raynas right here."

"And let me guess," said Anders, "you two are seeing three other Ellukkas and three other Lisabets."

They both nodded.

"This is perfect," Anders said, excitement building. "They'll all look into the mirror, and they'll all see themselves. Who do they trust more than themselves? Who do any of them think is smarter than themselves?"

With a soft popping sound, the effect ended, and suddenly he was looking at his friends once more.

"It didn't last very long," Lisabet said, her brow creasing.

"We'll have to hope that's what needs fixing about it," Anders said. "Maybe the dragonsmiths Drifa told us about, Tilda and Kaleb, can help. She said Hayn could too."

"Or maybe the Staff of Reya will do something," Lisabet suggested. "I wish we knew what it was for."

"I just hope it's in one piece," said Ellukka, "not four, like the Sun Scepter."

"There's only one way to find out," Rayna said, "but let's eat our sandwiches while we look at the map again."

They wrapped the mirror up and set it aside, then laid out the map once more.

This time Anders pricked his finger, squeezing a drop of blood onto the compass rose and speaking carefully. "We would like to find the Staff of Reya."

Rayna tied a bit of cloth around his finger, and as she did so, the knotwork around the edge of the map rearranged itself once more, presenting them with their next riddle.

"At end of day, it's always best
To find a place to take some rest.
At Dragons' Home, my place I make,
And there the staff my blood can take."

"What?" said Rayna, blinking at it.

"Well, by my blood, she means us," said Anders. "She means her relatives, her descendants."

"And by Dragons' Home, she means Drekhelm,"

Ellukka said. "That's what Drekhelm means in Old Vallenite."

Anders's stomach dropped. "How are we supposed to get into Drekhelm?" he asked. "That place is absolutely stuffed full of dragons, and they all must think we're their enemy by now, since we haven't showed up to celebrate what happened to Holbard and offer to do it anywhere else they want."

But Lisabet was shaking her head. "I don't think we have to go to Drekhelm," she said.

"But that's what—" Ellukka began, but she stopped as Lisabet shook her head again.

"Drifa wrote this before the last great battle," she said, "and before the last great battle, the dragons didn't live at Drekhelm."

"Oh, you're right," Ellukka said slowly. "They moved to Drekhelm because the wolves discovered where Old Drekhelm was."

"Right," Lisabet agreed. "So when Drifa wrote about Drekhelm in this puzzle, she meant what we call Old Drekhelm."

Anders considered this. "So we need to go to Old Drekhelm and figure out where she slept? And that's where the staff will be? Is it as big as New Drekhelm?"

Ellukka nodded. "Maybe even a little bigger," she said.

Anders groaned, and Rayna bit into her sandwich with feeling.

"At least it's not full of dragons," Lisabet ventured.

"We still have some of the day left," Ellukka said. "We'd better get going."

CHAPTER TEN

I T TOOK MOST OF THE DAY TO REACH OLD
Drekhelm. They flew northeast, skirting Cloudhaven
and flying above the village of High Rikkel, and past the
top of Lene's Pass, which linked the village to Port Alcher
down on the coast, before they veered east.

Anders could feel how tired Rayna was by the time
they arrived, the strokes of her wings taking that much
more effort, her head a little lower. But she lifted it as Old
Drekhelm came into sight.

High in the craggy peaks in the northmost reaches of
the Icespire Mountains, they saw the huge, gaping maw
of an opening. Ellukka flew confidently toward it—she
had been here before, though long ago—and Rayna fell
in behind her.

They landed in an enormous, dimly lit cave with a
cold wind blowing through it. Once more they removed

the girls' harnesses, pushing them off to the edge of the cave and into the shadows in case the wind picked up, and they transformed back to human form.

"There used to be big doors," Ellukka said, pointing at the opening to the cave mouth. "This was the Great Hall, just like at New Drekhelm, but they took the doors off and brought them with them."

"I suppose it's not the sort of thing you'd want to make twice if you didn't have to," Rayna observed.

The farthest recesses of the cave were completely hidden in the dark, but Anders could see it was much bigger than the Great Hall at New Drekhelm. For a moment, he imagined it full of people and dragons, lights and even dancing, as they had seen the night of the equinox. And then it was empty once more, sending a shiver down his spine.

"This place is huge," Rayna continued. "How are we possibly going to find out where she used to sleep?"

"Well, at least there are lamps," Ellukka said, walking over toward the entrance to unhook four of them from the collection that had been left there long ago. "They're dusty, but it looks like they still work, so we don't have to wander around in the dark. Oh, and"—she looked up, concerned—"someone's been here. There are footprints."

"You came once, with the Finskólars," Rayna pointed

out. "Maybe someone came visiting again?"

"We came a long time ago," Ellukka agreed, "but the dragons just fought a battle against the wolves, so the Finskólars at New Drekhelm aren't going to be out on class excursions right now. They've all got bigger things to deal with. And we know most of them are back at Cloud-haven. These footprints look recent."

"We'll have to hope it was just someone who was curious," said Anders.

"Or someone who just remembered last week that they left something behind when they moved out ten years ago," Rayna replied, in a voice that wanted to be cheerful but sounded a little bit unsettled.

"I think I know where the bedrooms were," said Ellukka, "but there are a lot of them, and I'm not sure how we'll know which one was Drifa's."

"All we can do is look," said Lisabet. "Lead the way."

Their lamps held high, they followed Ellukka down an empty hallway, their footsteps echoing without rugs to absorb them.

At New Drekhelm, artifact lamps would have come to life ahead of them, fading out slowly behind them, rendering the whole place in a cheerful yellow glow. Here, the dark seemed to close in from all directions.

Ellukka hesitated a couple of times, but a few minutes

later, she was gesturing triumphantly. "This hallway is where the bedrooms start," she said. "Why don't Lisabet and I go to the other end, and you two can hunt along here? If anyone sees anything, or thinks maybe Drifa slept in that room, they can shout. We'll hear."

"The sooner we start, the sooner we finish," Lisabet said. "Or, I guess, if it doesn't go well, then the sooner we know we need a new plan. Let's go."

She and Ellukka lifted their lamps high and made their way down the corridor, disappearing around a corner and leaving the twins alone.

"Let's get to work," said Rayna, sticking her head inside the first bedroom.

Anders took the bedroom across the hallway, holding up his lamp as he peeked inside. There was a bedframe carved into the rock, but apart from that, it was completely empty. He quickly studied the walls, but nothing was carved there, and there was no sign to show that anyone in particular had slept here, let alone Drifa.

He made his way through into the bathroom, but it was just as empty of anything helpful. *Maybe Drifa's room won't be this empty,* he thought. *She wasn't here to clear it out when the dragons left Drekhelm. She was already . . . missing. She was already wherever she is now, perhaps.*

He tried the next room, and the next, and the next after that, with no luck at all. As he and Rayna worked their way down toward the corner, Anders was beginning to appreciate what a very, very long task this might be, and to wonder if they should bring more reinforcements from Cloudhaven in the hope that more pairs of eyes could search the rooms more quickly.

He left the room he was in and was about to turn the corner to head along to the next door. But before he could, someone else came striding around it instead.

It was Leif, the head of the Dragonmeet, and the leader of the Finskól.

His old teacher's mouth fell open in surprise as they stood face to face for an instant, staring at each other. Then the Drekleid lifted one big hand, and without a word, he pushed Anders straight into the room Rayna was busy searching.

She turned around, her mouth open to ask what he was doing, and Anders frantically signaled to her to stay quiet as he hurriedly pushed across the shutter on his lantern to dim its glow. She closed her mouth again with a snap and followed his lead, dimming her own light and dashing over to join him as he peeked through the crack where the door's hinges joined it to the rock.

Leif was still there, turning his head to speak to someone over his shoulder. For a moment, he reminded Anders of Hayn. Not because he *looked* like Hayn—where his uncle's skin was dark brown, Leif's was a pale white, though ruddied and freckled by the sun, and where Hayn's hair was a tightly curled black, Leif's hair and beard were a much lighter red. But they both shared the same smile lines around their eyes, and both gave the impression that though they were large, they were gentle. And they had both protected him at different moments. They both felt like safety—even if one of them had just shoved him into a dark room.

Then Anders saw who Leif was speaking to. Around the corner came Valerius, Ellukka's giant blond father, and Torsten, whom Anders had always secretly called Bushy Beard. Then came two women that Anders recognized from the Dragonmeet, though he didn't know their names; then, finally, came Mylestom and Saphira, the two youngest members of the Dragonmeet. Mylestom was walking beside Saphira as she propelled her wheeled chair along.

Rayna held on to Anders's arm with an iron grip as they watched the procession pass by, as though she was trying to hold in all the questions she wanted to ask, and the things she wanted to say.

"I think we may as well go," Leif was saying. "There's nothing more we can do here today."

"If we can't find anything here that will help us," said Torsten, "then we should go ahead with what we have. There'll never be a better time."

"He's right," Valerius said grimly. "The wolves can't stay out there in that camp of theirs forever. They'll run out of things to eat."

"The humans will capitulate," said one of the women. "What else can they do?"

"That might be," said Saphira from behind them, "but there are still other options."

Anders held his breath, hoping against hope that neither Lisabet nor Ellukka would spot anything interesting enough at this moment to cause them to yell for the others to come join them. He and his sister extinguished their lamps completely and crept after the dragons as they made their way back to the abandoned Great Hall. Together, the twins hid in the shadows by the entrance as, one by one, the dragons began to transform.

After Valerius, Torsten, and the two women left, Saphira maneuvered her chair into the center of the hall and began to wheel it toward the ledge, Mylestom following behind her.

It was then that Leif raised his voice. "I think the two

of you should wait here a moment longer," he said. They both turned, curious, and he spoke again. "Anders? You'd better come out. And your sister too. I'm sure if you're here, she's somewhere close by."

Anders's breath caught, and he felt Rayna's hand tighten on his arm again. But Leif knew they were there. And even after all that had happened, Anders had no reason to mistrust his teacher. He had just hidden them from the unfriendly members of the Dragonmeet. And in the great battle above Holbard, Leif had defended his students.

So, slipping his hand into Rayna's, he walked out with his sister until they reached the circle of lamplight where Leif, Mylestom, and Saphira stood.

Leif hurried forward to meet them. "Are you both all right?" he asked. "Are you safe?"

"We were so worried," Saphira said, wheeling toward them quickly.

"And *what* was that you unleashed above Holbard?" Mylestom said. "None of us had ever seen anything like it."

Anders opened his mouth, then shut it again, not sure how much to admit or where to begin.

"We're not going to tell anyone we saw you," Leif said, glancing across at the other two, who nodded. "Let me guess: you're not here alone."

Anders exchanged a look with Rayna. There was no point trying to hide it, and he wasn't even sure they had a reason to.

Rayna walked back toward the entrance to the hallways and called out for Ellukka and Lisabet to come join them. They weren't long in arriving, coming at a run, and they both stopped short when they saw the three members of the Dragonmeet. Relief was written all over Ellukka's face as she walked forward. Lisabet looked almost as happy.

"Oh, Leif, it's good to see you," Ellukka said. "How's . . ."

"Your father's healing," Leif said, and her shoulders dropped as some of the tension went out of her. Though she knew he'd survived his injuries—thanks to Leif catching him as he fell above Holbard—she hadn't had any news since that first day she'd returned to Drekhelm with Theo to steal books from the archives.

"We saw him just now," Anders added. "He was walking."

"His burns are nasty," said Saphira, "but he can fly."

"And how are things at Drekhelm?" Rayna asked.

There was a long pause before Leif replied. "Complicated," he said eventually. "Some of the dragons are angry, some feel betrayed. Some want to attack Holbard. Others want to cut off all contact with the outside." He paused, and when he continued, his voice was grim. "I'm losing control of the Dragonmeet."

His words were met with a shocked silence. All four of the children had seen Leif at the head of the Dragonmeet, and though the adults argued and debated endlessly, in the end, they always listened to him.

"What were you doing here?" Anders asked.

"We were looking for weapons," Saphira said quietly. "Though we are very divided on whether or not we should use them. We thought we should at least come, so we knew if they found anything."

"And you?" Leif asked. "What brings you to Old Drekhelm?"

"We're looking for the place where our"—Anders caught himself in time and changed the words he had been about to use—"where Drifa used to sleep."

Mylestom's eyebrows went right up. "Drifa the dragonsmith? Why?"

None of the children answered him—nobody wanted to lie, but nobody was quite prepared to tell the truth, either. They all trusted Leif, Mylestom, and Saphira, but it was difficult to know whether—in an attempt to keep the peace—the adults might feel it was better to share something the children didn't want them to share.

"We're not here looking for a weapon," said Anders eventually. "I promise."

Leif nodded slowly. "I think I remember where her room used to be, but she was gone even before the dragons left Drekhelm. Her things might have ended up anywhere."

"You show them," said Saphira, "and we'll follow the others home. We shouldn't let them spend more than a few minutes at Drekhelm without at least one of the three of us there."

"She's right," said Mylestom. "Don't be too long, Leif."

With a nod of farewell to the children, the two of them made their way toward the great gaping mouth of the cave, Saphira wheeling her chair up to the edge of it as Leif led the children away.

"What does she do with her chair?" Lisabet asked curiously.

"She takes off," said Leif, "and then Mylestom picks it up and carries it if she'll need it at the other end. She has several, so often one is waiting for her. This way, come."

He led them through the dark corridors of Old Drekhelm, and as they made their way past the rooms they had already searched, Anders realized Leif might be able to answer another question for them.

"Did you ever know two dragonsmiths called Tilda and Kaleb?" he asked.

"Yes, I still know them," said Leif. "Their aerie's in the hermits' caves these days."

"Do you know where in the hermits' caves?" Lisabet asked immediately.

Leif nodded. "I can draw you a map. But Drifa's room is just up here."

He opened a wooden door that looked to Anders just like all the others, checked inside, and then opened it all the way.

The room was not empty like the others had been. When the dragons had fled after the last great battle, Drifa had already gone missing, and it seemed nobody had gathered up her belongings. There was a big, wide bed, some bookshelves at the end of the room—gaps here and there suggested these had been raided—and a large chest that sat open, a few pieces of clothing still inside it.

Anders's heart gave a little shiver. He walked into the room and across to the chest, leaning down to pick up a cloak. He held it in his hands, gazing down at the dark crimson fabric, running his fingertips over the metal catch at the neck. His mother had worn this. She had touched this with her own hands.

Rayna came up beside him and silently leaned her shoulder against his.

"Ah," said Leif quietly. "Yes. When I told you that I had my suspicions about how you had come to carry both wolf and dragon blood, this was what I wondered. I thought—I hoped—you might be her children."

"Really?" Rayna whispered, looking back at him. "You don't think it's wrong?"

Leif shook his head firmly. "My heart is glad to know my friend left something of herself behind. You should know that your mother was not a killer, Anders, Rayna. She never said it to me, but I knew that she loved Felix. I saw them working together, I could tell."

"We know she didn't kill him," Rayna said.

"Do you know who did?" Leif asked quickly.

"No," said Anders, lifting his head and making himself look around the room. "No, we don't."

And they didn't know what had happened to Drifa either. He found himself keeping quiet about that. If she didn't want her children to come and find her, he was somehow sure that she wouldn't want Leif or anyone else to try, either.

He couldn't see many places that a staff might be hidden, but he didn't want to search just yet. Not until Leif had left.

Seeming to understand, Leif spoke again. "Perhaps I can find something to draw a map on for you, to show you where to find the aerie."

"We have a map," Rayna said, digging it out of her bag and passing it over to Leif.

"This is Drifa's old map," he said, his brows shooting up. "Oh, I haven't seen this in . . . well, a very long time." He opened it up and, holding a lamp close, showed them the exact spot in the hermits' caves they should look. "You'll see a red flag flying outside the cave mouth," he said. "There's a big flat spot, and that's where you should land. Is there anything else I can tell you before I follow Saphira and Mylestom?"

"What happens if you lose control of the Dragonmeet?" Anders asked quietly.

"I don't think it's *if*," Leif said with a sigh. "I think it's *when*. The Dragonmeet will talk all day tomorrow about how we didn't turn up any lost weapons here, and in the old days, they'd have gone on talking for weeks after that. But some of them are getting ready to take action, and I think it could happen as soon as the day after tomorrow."

The children were silent for a moment, stunned. They'd known things were getting worse, but . . . the day after tomorrow?

"What will they do?" Ellukka asked quietly.

"Attack the wolves," Leif said, just as soft.

Anders felt sick just thinking about it. They couldn't let it happen. "Hayn said the wolves are training," he replied. "Everyone, even the junior students. Professor Ennar's in charge, and she was our combat teacher."

"Where's the Fyrstulf?" Leif asked, his brows lifting. "Where's Sigrid?"

"Nobody knows," Lisabet said tightly.

"Well, wherever she is," Leif replied, "and whatever she's out there doing, it'll make peace harder, not easier, that much I know. But this problem is much larger than Sigrid now. One way or another, I think we're only a day or two away from a war. You need to act quickly. I'll do my best to keep the Dragonmeet from doing anything foolish, but it's only a matter of time."

He clasped each of their hands in turn, and then took his leave, his footsteps echoing as he made his way down the hall.

The rest of them stood still, and Anders knew he wasn't the only one wishing that Leif could stay, could know everything they knew, could take charge. But that was impossible, and he gave himself a shake.

"Let's search," he said. "It shouldn't take long."

He and Ellukka took the bookshelves, since they were the tallest, reaching up to feel along the top with their hands and carefully checking behind them where they came away from the wall. Lisabet searched the dark corners of the room with her lamp.

Anders knew his friend had to be thinking about Leif's words.

Perhaps it was a comfort to her that he was so sure her mother was out there somewhere. Leif was right—the danger they were in was bigger than Sigrid, that was for sure. If the Dragonmeet was intent on war, then Sigrid herself could probably show up and tell everyone to hold hands and make friends, and it wouldn't be enough. But that didn't mean he wasn't worried about the Fyrstulf. He and Lisabet both knew that Sigrid was capable of causing a lot of trouble all by herself.

His thoughts were interrupted after a minute, when Rayna rolled completely under the bed and then squeaked in delight.

"Found it!" she called, then broke off into a fit of coughing as a cloud of dust emerged, followed by a gray and gritty Rayna.

"All of it?" Ellukka asked, hurrying over to help her to her feet.

"All of it," Rayna confirmed.

"Well, that's something," said Ellukka. "Sparks and scales, I was *not* looking forward to hunting all over Vallen for another three pieces."

Anders was already thinking ahead to the next step, and he lifted his lamp to look at the others. "Can we get to Tilda and Kaleb tonight?" he asked.

Ellukka and Rayna considered the question.

"I don't think so," said Ellukka. "It's a long way to fly when we're so tired. And how would we find the red flag in the dark?"

"And Drifa said we need Hayn," Lisabet pointed out. "So someone would have to fly to fetch him as well."

"It makes sense that we'd need a wolf designer to help with repairs," Rayna said. "She said that she and our father repaired the mirror together last time, so repairs must need a wolf and a dragonsmith."

"That's right," said Lisabet. "Of course, I should have thought of that. All around Holbard, artifacts were beginning to break this last year or two, because there weren't any dragonsmiths to help the wolves with repairs."

"The wind arches at the harbor," Anders said, remembering. "They kept letting in huge gusts."

"And lots of other small things besides," Lisabet agreed.

"Well," said Ellukka, "I hope Hayn likes the dragonsmiths as much as Leif does."

"We'll have to sleep here tonight," Lisabet said. "We'd have to fly to pick him up, and *then* fly to the caves, and he's going to be heavy. We're meeting him at the town camp tomorrow morning anyway. I know Leif said it was urgent, but it's too far and too dangerous to fly."

So they slept at Old Drekhelm, all four of them piling onto Drifa's bed. As Anders nestled his head down onto the pillow, he couldn't help but think that once, his mother had lain in this very place. Like being in her workshop, her bed brought with it a feeling of closeness. He wondered where she had slept when she hid at Drekhelm, and tried to imagine her lying in bed with her babies sleeping nearby.

She must have been aching with sadness for their father, who had been killed, and afraid that she would be found and blamed for something she hadn't done. She must have been afraid for Anders and Rayna as well. It must have been lonely.

Though neither he nor Rayna doubted their mother's innocence, now that he lay here in the dark, he couldn't believe he hadn't thought to ask her if she knew who *had* killed Felix when he'd had the chance. And now she was gone.

That thought brought with it a sadness that stayed with him late into the night.

CHAPTER ELEVEN

THE NEXT MORNING, ELLUKKA AND LISABET LEFT for the town camp to meet up with Hayn, promising to bring him to the hermits' caves as soon as they could. Anders and Rayna set off to find Tilda's and Kaleb's aerie.

They flew first over the Uplands, soaring above the broad, golden plains, watching the thousand streams that twisted and turned across them, mirroring the sky. Slowly, the perfect green carpet of the plains was broken up by small rocks, then large, and then they came to the foot of the Seacliff Mountains.

Rayna flew south of the Skylake, where they had found a piece of the Sun Scepter, wheeling through the passes that Hayn had shown them on the map, flying lower and more slowly, carefully hunting until they began to see the mouths of caves.

Then she dropped lower again, so the wind that was

twisting its way through the peaks began to buffet her this way and that. It was hard going, and it was another half hour before they saw a large red flag outside a cave mouth, fluttering fiercely in the breeze.

Beside it was a broad, flat platform, perfect for landing, and as Leif had told them to, Rayna set herself down in the very center of it.

No sooner had her feet touched the ground than a series of mechanical fences sprang up from where they had been concealed, forming a perfect circle around the landing pad. At first, they were perhaps six feet tall, and Rayna made as if to take off again and free herself from their enclosure. Then another layer of fencing seemed to unfold from the top of the first, and another from the top of that, expanding until, within seconds, the twins were enclosed in a large dome made of latticed metal.

Anders slowly slid down Rayna's side, putting down the package that contained the mirror, and then laying the staff on the ground beside it before he turned to pull off his sister's harness. There didn't seem much point in leaving it on when they clearly weren't going anywhere.

"What kind of welcome do they call this?" she demanded as soon as she was in human form. "I don't know about this place, Anders. There has to be another dragonsmith somewhere."

"Not one that will listen to us," he pointed out quietly.

Then a voice called to them from outside the fence. "Is that a harness? It looks very well designed. I like the strap that goes between your forelegs."

There was a woman standing and looking in at them. She had a large shock of curly silver hair and a long, square-jawed face, suntanned from being outside.

"Yes, it is," Anders called. "Can we come out, please?"

She considered this, tilting her head this way and that, studying them the way Isabina studied things through her microscope. "Who told you how to find us?" she asked.

"Leif," he replied.

Her rather stern face lit up. "Oh, Leif," she said. "Barely anyone else visits us. I suppose I should have known it was him." She hurried around the dome and pulled open a gate using a latch on the outside. "Leif sends us supplies. I don't suppose you have any for us?"

"Afraid not," said Rayna. "He sent us because we need a repair."

"Oh, a repair!" If anything, she seemed even more excited about this. "*Nobody* asks for those anymore. Come inside, come inside." She raised her voice to a shout. "Kaleb, we have visitors. They need a repair!"

Anders couldn't help wondering, as he followed her in,

whether the reason nobody ever came to see them for a repair was that nobody knew where to find them. But he kept his mouth shut.

Kaleb turned out to be an old man with very dark-brown skin and hair just as silver as Tilda's, cropped close to his head. His face was lined and wrinkled, and his expression gave nothing away as he looked them up and down.

"They're children," he pointed out, pressing a button in the wall near the cave's entrance.

With a series of clanks, the dome and fence folded back down into place, the gray of the metal disappearing against the rock once more.

"Leif sent them," Tilda told him, as though this excused their age.

"Well, what do you want?" he demanded.

"I'm sure they want food. Guests, Kaleb, we never have guests. We should feed them."

Kaleb made a dismissive noise, waving away her words with one hand. But despite the gesture, he stomped over to a cupboard against the wall, opening it to remove four plates and one of the most magnificent cakes that Anders had ever seen. It looked to have at least a dozen thin layers, and between each of them was a thick layer of jam.

"Wow," said Anders, who had not been expecting something that fancy to emerge from so plain a cupboard in the middle of the mountains.

"Kaleb made it," said Tilda proudly. "We have a lot of free time up here."

"Not enough else to do," Kaleb said crankily. "Now. Tell us what you want."

"This is the Staff of Reya," Anders said, holding it up. "And inside this cloth is the Mirror of Hekla, though last time we opened it up and looked into it, we all ended up . . ."

"Seeing everyone as yourself," Tilda finished for him. She and Kaleb had both gone quite still. "Where did you get these?" she asked.

"They used to be Drifa's," Anders hedged.

"Yes," said Kaleb pointedly, "we know that."

"Have you been stealing her things?" Tilda asked, all hints of friendliness now gone from her face. "How did you find these?"

"We used a map," said Rayna quickly, eager to defend them. "We . . ." She fell silent, and Anders knew she had suddenly realized that if these dragonsmiths knew how Drifa's map worked, then they would know that the twins were related to Drifa.

"No . . . ," said Tilda.

"It can't be . . . ," said Kaleb.

He put down the cake and stomped in closer. Both he and Tilda took a long, long look at each of the children's faces.

"And who is your father?" Tilda asked.

Anders knew this was where the greatest risk lay. But he wouldn't lie and trick them into helping. They were doing all this to try to convince the wolves and dragons and humans to tell each other the truth, and to listen, so he had to start as he meant to go on. He remembered again that he had seen Tilda's and Kaleb's names in the Skraboks—they had probably known both his parents.

"Our father was Felix," Anders said. "He was a wolf. And so am I."

Tilda brought one hand up to cover her mouth. "Oh, Felix," she said.

"We used to work with him and his brother," Kaleb said. "Good men."

"I never understood what happened," Tilda said. "They said that she killed Felix, and then ran. But the dragons hunted high up and low down, and they never could find her. I always wondered if whoever got Felix found her as well."

Anders and Rayna exchanged a long glance—they both wished they knew the same thing.

"Well," said Kaleb grimly. "If they did, looks like she got away for at least a little while, seeing as how you two are standing here in front of us. Protecting her babies would be a good enough reason to hide."

There was something about the way he spoke—gruff, but just a little careful—that made Anders wonder if Kaleb and Tilda knew that Drifa had kept a forbidden workshop at Cloudhaven, a place nobody dreamed she would go, so nobody thought to look.

If the two dragonsmiths had suspected, obviously they'd never shared that suspicion with anyone, and that made them allies.

Kaleb appeared to be finished with the subject, and he cut himself a slice of cake, biting into it with a vehemence that didn't invite questions. "These days, all we can do is forge," he continued. "We need a designer. These foolish battles got in the way of it. There hasn't been a new artifact in Vallen in ten years. Ten years! Do any of them think this was how it was supposed to be?"

"Well, um, good news," said Rayna. "Felix's brother, Hayn, is on his way. So you'll have a designer very soon."

"That's wonderful!" said Tilda.

"It's about time," said Kaleb.

"You two sit down and eat your cake," said Tilda. "We'll work out how to repair your artifacts when Hayn comes."

And so Anders and Rayna were both installed on a large, comfortable couch covered in a rug that didn't really stop the stuffing coming out of all the holes in it. They each obediently ate a large slice of cake, and sat quietly as the dragons returned to their forging.

Watching Tilda and Kaleb work was like watching a beautiful kind of dance. Tilda transformed effortlessly into a peach-and-gold dragon with wings like the sunset coming through the clouds, breathing dragonsfire infused with essence into her forge, golden sparks leaping from the white flames. Then she slipped back into human form and picked up a hammer, setting to work beating her metal out flat. Over and over, she repeated the steps, never faltering.

Kaleb was engraving a metal plate that he was working on. He had a very old, very battered chart pinned up on the wall, and he would consult it, carefully studying the runes, then engrave another of them before returning to the chart once more. The paper was singed around the edges and had clearly seen many years of use. It must have been designed before the last great battle.

Anders was entranced, and except that his cake had disappeared, he would have had no idea how much time had passed.

Then, outside, they heard a series of metal clangs as the dome snapped into place once more.

A moment later, they heard Hayn's voice shouting, half irritated, half amused. "Tilda? Kaleb? Let us out of this ridiculous contraption this minute!"

"Oh good," said Kaleb, setting down his tools and turning for the door. "Now we can get to work."

The twins followed the two dragonsmiths outside to find Hayn, Lisabet, and Ellukka trapped within the metallic dome, the two children looking much more concerned than the big wolf.

"Where have you been all this time?" Kaleb demanded as he stomped over to release the gate.

"You do know I can't fly?" Hayn asked, a smile playing across his lips as the enclosure folded itself down to disappear into the ground again. "How, exactly, did you expect me to get up a mountain? You could have come to fetch me, if you wanted me so badly."

Kaleb made a grunting noise and turned back inside. Hayn and Tilda exchanged a quick smile.

"I have more cake," said Tilda, "and there's milk

somewhere as well. Let's get you children settled. This might take a while."

"It can't take too long," Hayn said gravely. "Things are getting worse."

Anders thought of the Dragonmeet getting ready to launch an attack. Did Hayn know? "Worse?" he asked, dreading the answer.

"I've been keeping an eye on the wolf camp," Hayn replied. "A group of them went to speak to the humans, and the humans drove them out. With rocks, with sticks, with anything they could lay their hands on."

"Did the wolves fight back?" Lisabet whispered.

Hayn shook his head, but his expression was grim. "Not this time," he said. "Every wolf is taught never to harm a human. But a human's never harmed a wolf before. There's talk around the human camp that they need to be ready for a wolf assault, and there's talk around the wolf camp that they need to show up in force, to bring the humans into line."

"Do you think they'll do it?" Tilda asked, looking pale.

"I think all it takes is one human or wolf to begin it, and after that, I don't know who'll end it, or how," Hayn replied.

Everyone was silent, and Anders closed his eyes. It felt like all of Vallen was on a collision course—the dragons readying themselves to attack the wolves, the wolves and the humans preparing to fight each other.

"We don't have much time," he said.

"Not much at all," Hayn replied. "Tilda, Kaleb, we should get to work."

Anders, Rayna, Lisabet, and Ellukka squashed onto the couch together, and Tilda loaded them up with big glasses of milk and even bigger slices of cake. In whispers, they caught each other up on what had happened since they separated, and then slowly fell silent as they watched the designer and the dragonsmiths work together. It was the first time it had happened anywhere in Vallen in over a decade, and Anders found he was holding his breath as they quietly talked over each of the artifacts.

Tilda had been right. No matter how urgent the work, it did take a long time—they studied, they debated, and slowly but surely, they settled on the repairs they wished to make.

It wasn't just a case of re-engraving old runes. Hayn had to understand where and why the artifacts had begun to wear out, and create new combinations of runes that would reinforce them. The dragons would then need to forge the runes into place, taking care that each one was located exactly where it was required.

Some hours later, Anders was woken by Hayn, who was crouching in front of him and gently touching his knee.

"We're ready," the big wolf said, adjusting his glasses as he studied both Anders and Rayna, who was still waking up.

"Do you understand how these work?" Tilda asked from behind him. "They're powerful."

"We looked in the mirror last time, and it worked," Rayna said.

"You won't need to look in it this time," Tilda replied. "Keep it wrapped up, and when you're ready to use it, just unwrap it. Anyone who's within, say, fifty feet of it, maybe more, will feel its effects. What about the staff? Do you know how to use that?"

The children all shook their heads.

"What are you doing," grumbled Kaleb, "gallivanting around Vallen with artifacts you don't know how to use? What Drifa would have had to say about that, I don't know."

Hayn snorted. "Drifa and Felix and I were always creating artifacts out of nothing. Half the time, we had no idea what they were going to do until they did it. I think Drifa would say that her blood runs strong in these two."

The children all exchanged a long glance, but they kept quiet. It wasn't the time to tell the dragonsmiths that Drifa had *told* them where to find the mirror and the staff. That would raise far more questions than it answered, and they had to focus on using them to try to start peace talks, before their time ran out. Thankfully, neither of them had thought to ask how Anders had known which artifacts to ask the map to show him.

Hayn pointed at the staff. "When you're ready to use this one, take the end of it and drag it along the ground until you've drawn a circle. It doesn't matter whether you can see the circle. You can draw it over rock, over grass, anything you like. Anyone who steps inside it, their elemental powers will be completely neutralized. They won't be able to breathe flame or cast ice. They won't be able to transform."

"At all?" Ellukka asked. "They'll be humans?"

"Might do some of them good," Tilda said.

Anders's mind was racing. Already he could feel a plan beginning to form—he was starting to see what Drifa had thought of when he and Rayna had told her what they needed to do.

"Like I said," growled Kaleb, "it's powerful stuff. Are you sure you can handle it?"

"No," said Anders honestly, "but we'll try our best."

"Good." Kaleb gave him an approving nod. "That's the first sensible thing you've said. If you know how hard it is to control, you've been paying attention."

"We'd wait if we could," Anders replied. "But we don't have a choice. Hayn says the humans and the wolves could begin a battle any moment. And Leif said the dragons could attack by tomorrow."

"He what?" Hayn said, pulling off his glasses and pinching the bridge of his nose. "How did you manage to see—no, that's not the point. This is even worse than I knew."

"This is why we live up in the mountains," Tilda said. "This is how it was years ago, before your parents died. Only then it wasn't the dragons trying to start something, it was the wolves making demands for repairs that nobody could meet."

"They wanted to oversee our every move," Kaleb agreed. "What happened to Drifa and Felix wasn't the reason for all of it, it was the last straw. Sigrid was determined to have a fight."

"Do you think she could be behind this now?" Lisabet

asked, her voice so soft she was almost inaudible. Hayn shot her a pained look, and Anders slipped his hand into his friend's and squeezed.

"I don't know," Tilda replied. "But I think that with or without the Fyrstulf, these dragons, wolves, and humans will find any excuse they can to start fighting one another."

Hayn nodded. "Sigrid was a squad commander back at the time of the last great battle, and though she pushed the pack toward war, I don't believe she was the cause of it. She was just a symptom of something much larger."

Anders glanced across at Lisabet, who was studying her shoes with a miserable expression.

"That wolf will never settle for peace," Tilda said with a sigh. "You mark my words. But Hayn's right. The elementals—and now the humans too—don't need Sigrid to find a way to fight. Perhaps we were wrong to hide up here in the mountains. Perhaps we should have done more."

"You've done it now," Anders said. "You've repaired the artifacts for us."

"We've picked a side, all right," Kaleb agreed. "Now make sure you win."

Tilda was absentmindedly collecting their empty milk glasses as they all spoke, when she paused and leaned in over Kaleb's shoulder to take a closer look at Anders.

"What's that?" she asked, pointing. "What's that around your neck?"

"They're Drifa's and Felix's old augmenters," said Hayn. "Both the children have one."

But Tilda shook her head. "They're more than that," she said, gesturing to Anders. "Give it to me for a minute."

Anders pulled his augmenter off over his head and passed it to her. He was surprised how urgently he wanted it back, though, like it had become a part of him. He was used to having it around his neck now.

"This is a key," she said, turning it over in her hand and passing it to Kaleb, who nodded confirmation.

"A key to what?" Rayna asked.

"No idea," said Kaleb. "Do you want anything else, or are you leaving now?"

"This has been a lot of company for one day," Tilda said, pressing one hand over Kaleb's mouth to silence him.

In the end, Tilda said that she would drop Hayn back near the town camp so the children could head straight to Cloudhaven. Not that she knew where they were going— she didn't ask, and they didn't mention it.

They were grateful for the extra time to fly, though. They had a lot of work to do on their final plans, and according to Leif and Hayn, they had to be ready by tomorrow. That urgency was bearing down on all of them, and Anders and Lisabet climbed up onto the girls' backs in tense silence.

The flight was longer than it needed to be, because a direct line would have taken them far too close to New Drekhelm for anyone's comfort. Instead, they dipped south to avoid it, flying over the Great Forest of Mists.

Glancing down over Rayna's shoulder, Anders remembered the first time he had run through the forest, the time he had tumbled into the river, to be pulled out by Lisabet. It had been the moment that had cemented their friendship forever. He looked across at her where she was hunkered down on Ellukka's back to stay out of the wind, and wished he knew the right thing to say, that he could take away her worries and her guilt over her mother.

Dusk arrived long before they reached Cloudhaven, turning the mist beneath them a golden pink. By the time they reached the rocky spire itself, night had long since fallen, and the sky above them was scattered with silver stars. They'd napped while the dragonsmiths and Hayn worked, and Anders was glad of it—no doubt most of their friends would be asleep by now.

Bryn and Det were sitting by the archway through to the entrance hall, talking quietly and keeping watch for the four of them, and Anders waved as he slid down

Rayna's side. A tiny dark shadow—Kess the cat—jumped out of Det's lap and came running over to greet them.

Anders leaned down to run one hand along her silky back, but Rayna twisted her head around, hitting him with a blast of hot dragon breath as she rumbled impatiently at him.

"Sorry, Kess," he whispered. "Just a minute."

No sooner had he pulled his sister's harness away than she threw herself into human form, grabbing for his hand.

"Anders, I've got it!"

"Got what?" he asked, but she was already towing him toward the entrance, Lisabet and Ellukka hurrying to keep up.

"It's a key!" Rayna crowed. "Bryn, just the dragon I need!"

"Welcome home?" said Bryn, her brows raised.

"Rayna, what's going on?" Anders tried, as she pulled him through the arch.

"It's a *key*," Rayna repeated, and he gave up, simply following her. There was no point in arguing with Rayna when she was in a mood like this. It was best just to hope she wasn't leading him headlong toward anything too disastrous.

"Are we going somewhere?" Lisabet asked.

"You'd better come, you're clever," Rayna decided.

"And Bryn, we need you. Ellukka and Det, you two tell everyone we won't be long. I don't think."

"You'd better not be," Ellukka replied. "We have a war to stop."

"I think," said Rayna, "this might be almost as important."

CHAPTER TWELVE

THEY WEREN'T SUPPOSED TO HEAD INSIDE CLOUD-haven without being part of a large group, and four was not a large group. But Rayna had let go of Anders's hand and was already hurrying ahead, so there was nothing to do but run after her.

As Anders jogged along the hallway, though, his ears were straining, listening for noises, for any sign that an artifact warrior might be on the move.

Rayna took the turns quickly and confidently, and he realized where she was leading him just a few moments before the final corner brought them to their destination.

She came to a halt, the others panting behind her, in front of the huge stone wall that had blocked their way when they had asked Cloudhaven how they could reach Drifa. The same text as always was still glowing at them, the words in Old Vallenite and the mysterious code.

The blue letters made no more sense than they ever had. Anders looked at Rayna, and she pulled her augmenter off over her head.

"Bryn, remember how you said that if we were going to decode the message on the wall, we need a key?" she said.

Bryn nodded, her brow creasing in confusion.

"Well," Rayna said, grinning, "you were right. Only I think what we need is an actual *key*. We met two dragonsmiths last night, Tilda and Kaleb, and—"

"You *met* Tilda and Kaleb?" Bryn gasped. "They're hidden in the mountains, they never let anybody land there, how did you . . . ?"

"Leif told us the way," Rayna replied.

"You saw *Leif*?"

"We have a lot to catch you up on," Rayna admitted. "And we will, as soon as we've done this. Tilda and Kaleb told us that our augmenters were keys, but they didn't know what for. I think they might belong *here*. Drifa herself said we're descended from the founders of Cloudhaven, and these augmenters used to belong to her. Sounds to me like it could unlock a door at Cloudhaven, and this is the only one we haven't been able to open."

The other three sprang to life, working quickly to search every inch of the stone wall. Anders ran his fingertips carefully over its rough surface, desperate to hurry but careful to make sure he didn't miss even the smallest opening.

It was Lisabet who called out first. "Here," she said, pointing urgently to the spot, and stepping back so Rayna could reach it.

It was a small, vertical slot, concealed in the shadow of a craggy piece of rock. Rayna turned her augmenter to match it and pushed it in.

It fit perfectly.

They all looked up at the rock wall, waiting for something to happen. But nothing changed.

"But it fits," Rayna protested, "that's the keyhole. Why isn't it working?"

Now, though, it was Anders's turn to have a hunch. He hurried down to the other end of the wall, searching at the same height. And sure enough, there was a matching keyhole.

He pulled his augmenter off over his head and, holding his breath, pushed it into place.

With a grinding noise, the glowing letters immediately began to change and shift, moving about on the rock wall. Whenever they met, they seemed to bounce off each other, like a crowd of people all trying to hurry in different directions, nobody willing to give way.

Eventually, though, a pattern began to emerge. The letters formed lines and clustered together into words.

"This is Old Vallenite," Bryn said, backing up and beginning to mutter to herself as she worked out the translation.

The other three danced, jumping up and down on the spot, unable to contain their celebration.

"I think I can translate it," Bryn said eventually. She haltingly began to read the words from the wall, line by line, first reading each in Old Vallenite, and then translating it.

"I am Cloudhaven.

I was made by the first of the dragonsmiths.

I will be known by the last of the dragonsmiths.

I will stand against wind and rain, against battle, against the shaking of the earth.

Those who have been granted my protection may roam me freely.

But only those with the keys of my founders may open this final door."

As she finished reading, a door began to form at the base of the huge stone wall. Lines of blue light glowed around its edges, and when its outline was complete, it opened with a soft click, swinging inward to reveal a staircase beyond it.

They all gazed at it in silence, and eventually Bryn spoke. "Should you go down there?" she asked. "I know you have to find out, but is it safe?"

"There's a bigger problem than that," Anders said, still looking down the stairs. "Leif and Hayn said the dragons, the wolves, *and* the humans are getting ready for another battle. We don't have long to use the staff and the mirror. But if things go badly, this might be the only chance we ever have to find out what happened to our mother. And it's not just for us. I think . . . I think it might be important for everyone to know. Her disappearance was mixed up in the start of the last great battle."

"We'll be back as quickly as we can," Rayna said.

"Let everyone else stay asleep," Lisabet said. "Whatever happens tomorrow, we're going to have a big day. We napped at Tilda and Kaleb's—we'll make sure we're back up here by morning."

"We?" said Anders.

She looked across at him. "You don't really think I'd let you two go alone, do you? We'd better hurry."

"I'll be waiting for you when the sun comes up," Bryn promised. "Right now, I'm going to run all the way back to the entrance hall, just to be sure I don't meet any unfriendly artifacts. You three go. Find Drifa."

They watched her to the corner, and then the twins retrieved their augmenters, hanging them around their necks once more. Silently, the trio began to descend the stairs, moving slowly at first, and then gathering speed as they became more confident.

They were about twenty stairs down when the door above them swung shut with a click.

Anders's heart stopped for a moment as he stood there in the dark. And then the soft greenish-blue glow of the paths that led them around Cloudhaven began to emanate from the walls.

So down and down and down they went, seeming to descend the stairs endlessly until Anders's feet hurt and the muscles in his legs ached. But they couldn't leave this mystery unsolved. The path that had promised to show them Drifa's location had led them to this wall. Drifa was down here somewhere, and though she had told them not to come, they could do nothing else.

Eventually, Anders began to wonder how they were going to get back up again. Even if they climbed all the stairs—and he was beginning to think they were descending all the way down to ground level—would they be able to open the door from the inside?

But his thoughts were interrupted by a distant noise.

He couldn't quite tell what it was, only that he had heard something, and he knew by the sharp turning of Rayna's head and the way Lisabet paused that they had heard it as well.

They continued down, but they moved more slowly now, careful to keep their footfalls silent. He trailed one hand along the cool rock beside him, wishing he could communicate with Cloudhaven more clearly. Wishing it could tell him what was waiting for him.

When they reached the bottom of the stairs, they emerged through an archway into the largest cavern Anders had ever seen. At first, he didn't know what he was looking at. Then, by the dim light that glowed from the ceiling, he began to understand.

He was seeing row after row after row of artifact warriors, all standing to attention, staring straight ahead. There were hundreds of them, maybe even thousands, the rows stretching away as far as he could see. The air vibrated with the same tingle that Anders always felt when an artifact that he was holding activated.

"What is this place?" Rayna whispered, but Anders had no answer.

Lisabet pointed up at the ceiling, keeping her voice as soft as she could. "Look, there are hatches up there. Remember when you locked the warrior in that room, and then it vanished through that trapdoor in the floor? This must be where it ended up."

They waited in silence for a little, but there was no sign of life anywhere. So eventually, they began to creep forward.

Every part of Anders was on edge as they made their way between the warriors, but none of them stirred or gave the slightest sign that they knew the children were there.

Lisabet nudged him, and when he looked where she nodded, he realized that some way away, perhaps at the center of the room, there was a brighter glow. There was something there.

They altered course toward it, still keeping their footfalls silent, every sense awake and searching for danger.

The temperature began to drop as they approached the middle of the room, and the wolf in Anders knew without question that this was an ice wolf's work.

With matching intakes of breath, the twins stopped short as they saw what was causing both the cold and the glow. A step behind them, Lisabet bumped gently into Anders, then gasped.

In front of them was a huge block of ice, nearly a hundred feet high and a hundred feet across. Suspended at the very center of it was a dragon, a deep red with glorious bronze undersides to her wings, reared up on her back legs as if to breathe flame at someone.

Anders stared. It couldn't be . . .

Could it?

"It's her," Rayna breathed. "It has to be."

All their lives, the twins had wondered about their mother. Where she'd gone, why she'd left them. Until they'd found Cloudhaven they'd always believed she'd died in the last great battle, but a tiny part of Anders had still dreamed of meeting her.

He could scarcely believe that she was here, right in front of them. So close, yet impossible to touch.

Lisabet squeezed his hand gently. "What are those?" she whispered.

When he tore his attention away from where his mother was encased in the ice, he saw what looked like ropes—they seemed to be attached to Drifa, emerging from the ice block and snaking away into the dark. But when he crouched to look at one more closely, he saw that they were made of metal.

He followed it from its source out into the dark, and discovered that it stretched in a perfectly straight line, a long row of artifact warriors standing on top of it.

Then Anders knew what he was seeing.

"She's powering them," he said softly. "Our blood has essence in it, and the essence in hers is powering the artifact warriors."

"But she can't be controlling them," Rayna protested. "They attacked us. She'd never do that."

"No, I don't think she is," Anders said. "She couldn't have frozen herself in the ice. Someone did this to her. The question is, can we get her out?"

"I'll follow one of the ropes to the end," Lisabet volunteered. "See if there's anything I can learn about it."

"Be careful," Anders said.

"Oh, don't worry, if one of the warriors moves, you'll hear me screaming about it."

She slipped off into the darkness, and the twins stood side by side, each absorbed in their own thoughts.

Anders lost track of time, but he was just beginning to wonder where Lisabet was when a voice broke the silence behind them.

"What are *you* doing down here?"

He spun around, Rayna a moment behind him, and found himself face to face with Sigrid—the Fyrstulf, the head of Ulfar, the leader of his pack, and Lisabet's mother.

She looked almost as she always had, with her very white skin and her pale-blond hair. But her Ulfar uniform was filthy, and there was a smear of dirt across one cheek, a hint of wildness in her eyes.

The children stared at her in disbelief.

Sigrid.

All this time spent wondering where she was, wondering if she was alive at all, watching Lisabet try to hide her own fears while they all worried about what her mother was going to do next . . . and here she was beneath Cloudhaven itself, standing next to the twins' mother and telling *them* to explain themselves?

Something inside Anders exploded, a swirling mix of surprise, anger, and fear pushing to the surface. "What are *we* doing here?" he echoed. "What are *you* doing here? Did you do this to Drifa?"

"I needed her power," Sigrid said, glancing past them at Drifa without a trace of guilt. She spoke as if it were the most obvious thing in the world. "The artifact warriors are the answer, and she was an incredible dragonsmith. Her blood can do things nobody else's could. The warriors can fight for us. I've already been teaching them to attack."

"Is that what they're for?" Anders asked, feeling like someone was squeezing his chest. There were thousands of the warriors all around them. "Were they designed to fight?"

Sigrid waved a dismissive hand. "The founders had no imagination. They're for assistance. Maintenance. Whatever they are required to do. Now, they are required to fight. They can move anywhere within Cloudhaven—I can't get through the door at the top of the stairs, but they allowed me glimpses of you. And more to the point, the warriors can march out into Vallen with enough power."

"How could you?" Rayna asked, her voice breaking. "Is this where Drifa's been all this time?"

"She deserved worse," Sigrid said, with a horrible matter-of-factness. "I never believed the collaboration with the dragons was wise. They're unreliable, unpredictable. Undisciplined. But it was necessary, though we always had to treat them with caution. Dragons have never been trustworthy. This one, though . . ." And now her expression hardened. "I found her with a wolf. There was something wrong with her. With both of them."

"There was nothing wrong with them," Rayna snapped. "They were in love!"

"That's not possible," Sigrid shot back. "He was a fool, and a traitor to his pack. The two of them claimed to have grand ideas about a peace, a truce, but she was deceiving him. No dragon has ever believed in peace. If we'd let our guard down, they would have had the victory they'd wanted for so long."

"Did you . . . ?" Anders could hardly bring himself to ask it. A part of him didn't want to hear the answer, and a part just as painful knew that Lisabet must be out there listening to them. "Did *you* kill the wolf?"

"He defied me," Sigrid replied, and though she didn't say it, the unspoken answer was perfectly clear: *yes*. "But in death, he served our pack. He showed everyone that the dragons weren't to be trusted."

"What do you mean?" Rayna spluttered. "You wanted them to hand Drifa over for a trial, but *you* were the guilty one! And she couldn't tell anyone the truth, you'd trapped her here."

"Please," Sigrid replied, rolling her eyes—as if Rayna were being hysterical, as if she needed someone calm to explain the truth to her. "The dragon always wanted war. She was taking advantage of him to learn about the wolves. If she loved him, why did she abandon him? Her plan had failed, and she fled."

Anders blinked at his old pack leader, and Rayna caught her breath.

"You don't know," Anders said quietly.

"Know what?" Sigrid's voice was sharp.

"She didn't run until you'd killed him," Anders said. "But then she had to. She had to protect her children."

Now it was Sigrid's turn to gasp, her pale-blue eyes

wide with horror. "Her *children*? Children of a wolf and a dragon?"

"Hi," said Anders. "Pleased to meet you."

Sigrid took a quick step back, as if he might be somehow infectious. "You have dragon blood in you," she whispered. "And we let you inside Ulfar?"

"We let him inside Drekhelm too," said Rayna, folding her arms across her chest. *And your daughter as well*, she might have said, but like Anders, she let Lisabet remain quietly in the shadows. Sigrid's daughter would speak when she wanted to. *If* she wanted to.

"The silver flame," Sigrid realized slowly. "That was icefire. I couldn't understand how it was created. It's only ever been a theory."

"Not anymore," Rayna replied. "All we've ever wanted is peace. All you've ever done is fight for war, from before we were even born. You killed our father, you trapped our mother here."

"You tried to rule Holbard through fear," Anders said. "And when that didn't work, you lit fake fires so people would be scared of dragons who weren't even there. You've been waiting to take charge of the whole city, maybe the whole island, all this time."

"To keep us safe," Sigrid insisted. "Nobody's been paying attention. The wolves grow lazy, the humans don't listen, and the dragons will come. I refuse to cower out on the plains with the rest of the pack. I have survived here with nothing, sacrificing *everything* for this chance!"

She flung out one arm, and Anders followed her wild gesture—she was pointing at a makeshift camp back in the shadows, a blanket tucked in beneath a rock ledge, a single cooking pot, a small, dead fire.

"You've been down here since the battle," he realized.

"I knew I had to come back and finish what I once started," Sigrid replied. "I showed my pack the danger of the dragons once before."

"By killing our father and framing our mother!" Rayna shouted. "That was the danger of *you!*"

Sigrid continued as if she hadn't spoken. "They didn't listen. I fought my way up to Fyrstulf, the better to protect them. If they don't see it now, I'll take the fight to the dragons myself."

"The last great battle was because of you," Rayna said, her horror growing.

"We lost our parents," Anders said, "because of you."

"I did all this for you," Sigrid replied, her voice rising. "You were the next generation. You had to be protected. And how did you repay me? You filled my daughter's ears with lies, you betrayed our pack! I knew when I froze the dragonsmith that I could use her to power the warriors, to rule Vallen for its own protection, but I couldn't find the way. This time, I won't fail."

And now Anders saw clearly, with a pang for Lisabet that nearly broke his already bruised and damaged heart. "You're insane," he whispered.

"I'm the only one who sees the truth and is prepared to act on it," Sigrid whispered in reply.

In an instant she'd slipped into her wolf form, baring her teeth in a snarl as she slammed her paws down onto the ground. A sheet of ice began to ripple out from her at lightning speed, spreading across the cavern and into the distance, covering the floor.

And everywhere it reached, one by one, the warriors began to lift their heads.

CHAPTER THIRTEEN

THE ROWS OF ARTIFACT WARRIORS CAME TO LIFE, shifting and clicking as the ice reached them and gave them Sigrid's instructions.

An instant later the warriors were lumbering toward them, arms outstretched, unseeing faces turned toward the twins.

"Quick, transform!" Rayna cried, throwing herself into dragon form. She was far too big for the space, and she collided with rows of warriors as she grew in an instant. She trumpeted her defiance as she swung her tail at another row of them, sending them tumbling into one another with a series of crashes.

Anders was only a moment behind her, the ice all around them only strengthening him as he shifted.

I exiled you from the pack, Sigrid growled behind him. *You should have stayed away.*

Rayna swung her tail again, and Anders ran underneath her for shelter as the first warriors reached him, one leaning down to clumsily grab at him. There were so many of them—hundreds, thousands, and there was no way he could fight them all.

But his sister had nowhere to hide, and she bellowed in pain as the warriors began to swarm her, grabbing at her legs, one reaching up for her far more delicate wing.

It was that sound—her pain—that mobilized him. He ran out from beneath her with a snarl, launching a wave of icefire without a second thought, and sending a row of warriors tumbling backward. They lay still where they fell, their runes melted, their power gone.

But there were more behind them, and more behind *them.*

How long could the twins possibly hold on?

Another warrior made a grab at him, and he skittered sideways, then threw another gout of icefire toward it. He couldn't do this a thousand times—he'd exhaust himself, or one of them would grab him, and then . . .

Suddenly there was a howl from the far side of the cavern, and Lisabet was racing toward them. *The ice!* she howled to Anders, her ears up, her tail flying back and forth as if to propel her faster. *Melt the ice!*

He instantly turned his silver flame on the ice

surrounding his mother. A moment later Rayna joined him, not understanding their howled communication, but trusting the wolves.

Anders had seen chunks of ice fall from the cart of the ice man onto the streets of Holbard in the summer. On hot days, the street children ran after him and picked up the pieces that were left behind. The ones that weren't picked up, though, those pieces of ice shrank as the pools of water around them grew larger, and then, eventually, they were gone.

That happened now, the great square of ice dissolving, the dragon within it slipping lower and lower until she finally lay on the ground.

For a moment, she was perfectly still. And then she seemed to vanish.

It took Anders a moment to realize that she had simply shrunk from fifty feet in length to six. She was human again.

Her mop of curls lying wet around her still face, their mother was motionless on the rock.

And so were the warriors, their power source suddenly cut.

He, Rayna, and Lisabet shifted back to human form, three small figures amid a pile of debris that had once been an army of artifact warriors.

Sigrid transformed back to her human shape even as she ran forward, grabbing hold of two of the leads that were no longer connected to Drifa. She gritted her teeth, throwing her head back, the muscles in her neck taut as the outermost warriors began to power up again, the glow growing.

"Let go of them," Anders said urgently, "it will drain you dry."

In that moment, it was hard to care what happened to Sigrid, but he was thinking of Lisabet.

"She can't hear you," Rayna said quietly.

But Anders thought perhaps she could. She was staring at him, mouthing words he couldn't make out.

"Mother, stop!" Lisabet cried. "Please!"

Sigrid dropped to her knees, letting out a ragged breath.

"If you don't let go, it will kill you," Rayna insisted as noise began to start up all around them.

The warriors were beginning to move, flexing their arms and legs each in turn, as if stretching after a long rest.

"*Please!*" Lisabet sobbed, running over to grab her mother's arm, only to be thrown back by the force of the essence crackling through her now.

Sigrid had turned whiter than white.

"Let go!" Anders cried.

"I won't," she insisted through gritted teeth. "They have to be powered. Vallen *has* to be protected!"

But a moment later she did let go, her hands flexing and opening as she collapsed on the ground.

Anders kicked first one cord and then the other away from her, afraid to touch them with the bare skin of his hands.

Then he dropped to one knee, and leaned down to hold his fingers in front of Sigrid's slightly open mouth, afraid of what he would find.

No breath came from it.

He rose slowly to his feet, and—more reluctantly than he'd ever done anything in his life—he met Lisabet's eyes.

She gave a quiet cry of pain, and around them, the artifact warriors slowly began to settle once more, growing still, becoming silent.

For a very long moment none of the three elementals moved. Then there was a soft noise from nearby.

It was Drifa.

Anders was running toward her before he knew he was moving, and he dropped to his knees in the pool of water around her, carefully lifting her head to cradle it in his lap as Rayna took her hands.

Drifa's brown skin was tinted gray, and when her lashes fluttered, Anders saw that her brown eyes had been washed the palest of blue. But his heart soared to see her lashes move—she was alive, if only just.

She looked up at them, drinking in first his face and then Rayna's, and her lips moved to an exhausted smile.

"My darlings . . . ," she whispered.

"We're here," Anders told her, choking on a sob. "We're both here."

"We love you," Rayna murmured, her voice breaking.

"You have to finish it," Drifa managed. "What Felix and I tried to begin. What even Sigrid wanted, in her wrong, twisted way. There has to be peace."

"There will be," Anders promised. "We'll do it together."

"I know you will," she breathed. "Finish our work, then live happy lives, my darlings. I'm so proud of you. Your father would have loved every inch of you."

She let out a long, slow breath, and then she was still.

She was so completely motionless that Anders knew she was gone. His throat closed, and his heart beat too hard in his chest, and everything around him seemed to come into perfect focus. He could have counted his mother's eyelashes in that moment. He could have described every stitch of her clothes in perfect detail. He could have done anything, except speak the truth out loud.

His heart was breaking—his mother was gone, the leader of his pack's urge to protect those in her charge had pushed her to this. Everything was upside-down, and everything was wrong.

Sigrid was gone.

Drifa was dead.

CHAPTER FOURTEEN

THE CAVERN WAS QUIET ALL AROUND THEM, THE artifact warriors unmoving, the twins crouching by their mother. Lisabet stood near them, Sigrid still on the ground. Anders heard a soft dripping as the ice that had surrounded Drifa continued to melt, then a soft crack as a piece split away.

As if the sound had released her, Lisabet let out another sob, and without a word, both the twins gently laid down their mother, then walked over to fold their friend up in their arms.

"We'll come back," Anders said softly. At first, he meant it as a promise to their mother. But somehow, after a moment, he knew it was a promise to Sigrid as well. "We'll come back and get them both."

He didn't know where the right place would be to

lay either a wolf or a dragon to rest. But someone would know. And it wasn't here.

Their tears still flowing, the three of them turned, hand in hand, to find their way back to Cloudhaven once more. Ache though they might, they couldn't let their friends down. There was work to do, and not much time to do it.

* * *

Beyond Sigrid's makeshift bed they found a tunnel leading out to the mountains at the base of Cloudhaven. There, Rayna shifted to her dragon form, and Anders and Lisabet climbed up onto her back in silence. Anders wrapped his arms tightly around his best friend as his sister took off, launching herself up into the mist.

The dawn turned the world pink and gold as she beat her wings against the cool air, and Anders tried to let go of his sadness, at least for now, and focus on what the next few hours would hold. That was what Drifa had wanted him to do.

Sigrid would have wanted the war that might begin today, and if they didn't do everything exactly right, it would still happen just as she'd hoped.

As he, Rayna, and Lisabet made their way in through

the archway from the landing pad, they found their friends awake and debating what to do.

"Perhaps we should try to go after them," Det was saying.

"But how?" Isabina asked. "We don't have the keys."

"No need," Anders said, and though he was quiet, somehow they all heard him, swinging around and breaking out into exclamations of relief.

"Are you all right?" Ellukka asked, hurrying forward.

"What did you find?" Jerro asked.

"The answer to both of those is . . . complicated," Anders said. "And we'll tell you all of it later."

"For now," said Lisabet, her voice steady, "we have a war to prevent."

Ellukka studied her, head tilted to one side, as if she sensed something had happened to Lisabet. But then she nodded, and didn't press for details. "Let's eat breakfast and make a plan. We don't have much time."

Jai hurried back to the fire to begin filling bowls, but when Anders took his and looked up, he realized everyone was watching him. Waiting for *him* to make the plan. At least he'd had a little time to think on the way back from Tilda's and Kaleb's aerie.

"We can use the Staff of Reya to block their elemental

powers," he said, a part of him noticing that he didn't find it difficult to speak to the group anymore. He didn't find it difficult to . . . lead.

"And the mirror will make sure they all see the person they trust the most," Rayna said. "Themselves."

Sakarias frowned. "The problem is getting them all in the same place, at the same time, without any of them killing anyone before we can use the artifacts," he said. "That's going to be tricky."

"And dangerous," Mikkel agreed. But his voice was quiet, and calm. He wasn't refusing or backing away from the task. He was just stating a fact.

"It will be dangerous," Anders agreed. "If any of us are caught, I don't know what will happen. They'll imprison us, at best. Exile us, maybe, I don't know. The stakes for Vallen are even higher, though. If anyone doesn't want to be a part of this, I understand. One of the dragons can take you somewhere safe, maybe to a village somewhere."

Everyone around him was silent. Eventually it was Sam who spoke. "This needs all of us," he said. "And we're in."

"That's right," Jerro agreed. "Sam and I can find a way to get the mayor to the meeting spot. It'll need to be walking distance from the Holbard camp, though."

"I have some ideas," said Rayna, and Jerro shot her a

nervous look. Rayna's escapades were famous among the street children of Holbard.

"We'll need to be the ones who bring the Dragon-meet," Theo said. "We'll have to fly to Drekhelm."

Ellukka grinned suddenly. "And when we get there, we're going to offer them exactly what they want the most."

"What's that?" Anders asked.

She grinned wider. "You."

Sakarias and Viktoria were talking quietly, and looked up. "We can lead the wolves to a meeting," Viktoria said. "If they see us, they'll follow."

"Chase us," Sakarias corrected her, grinning.

"Let's not eat too much breakfast then," Jai said wryly. "We're going to need to be able to run *really* fast."

Ferdie was studying Anders. "Do you know what you're going to say when they all arrive, Anders?"

Anders blinked. "Me?"

There were nods all around the circle. He took a moment to think it over.

"I'll . . ." He studied his friends, and slowly it came to him. "Yes," he said. "I know what I'm going to say. I'm proud you're all my friends—wolf and dragon and human. I'm *honored* to be your friend. I'm going to find a way to show them all what this is like. The strength in it. I'm going to tell them about us."

*   *   *

Anders's thoughts were still whirling as Rayna launched from the landing pad at Cloudhaven, turning southeast to skirt the bottom of the Icespire Mountains and head across the Great Forest of Mists, crossing the Sudrain River and making for the spot near the Holbard camps that they had chosen for their meeting place.

For once, he barely noticed the view, and he couldn't bring himself to admire the beauty of the land below. He knew that soon he would have to find the words to explain everything that was in his head and his heart. He knew from the way Lisabet's arms tightened around his middle every so often that she was just as heartsore as he was, but as the wind flew by, there was no comfort he could offer her except to rest his hand on top of hers.

By the time Rayna landed and he pulled off her harness, he felt no more ready than he had at the beginning of the trip. But he was determined. He would find the right words. He *had* to find the right words.

They were in the foothills to the north of the ruins of Holbard, within walking distance of the town camp, running distance of the wolves' camp, and flying distance of Drekhelm. It was a large, fairly flat area, a little raised up, with a series of boulders off to one side.

Anders chose what he thought was the middle and set down the wrapped cloth package that held the Mirror of Hekla.

Meanwhile, Rayna took the Staff of Reya and began to trace out a large circle, just as Hayn had instructed them. She carefully dragged it over grass, dirt, and stone, making sure she didn't miss an inch, and that the edges of the circle connected up when she was finished.

And after that, there was nothing more they could do, except wait and hope.

The three of them settled into their hiding place between two of the boulders, and Anders opened up his communicator mirror to see how the others were doing. If anything went wrong now, then everything they were doing would have been for nothing.

Ellukka and Sakarias were equipped with two of the four communicators in Drifa's and Felix's set. Anders had the third, and Sam and Jerro had met Hayn just outside the humans' camp, taking the fourth from him.

Anders spoke Ellukka's name quietly into the communicator and waited for it to bring him an image from her point of view. She had her mirror pinned to the front of her cloak, like a brooch, so if anything went wrong they would at least be able to watch it and know what was happening.

The surface of the little mirror didn't change, though. It remained completely blank, showing Anders only his own reflection, which must mean that Ellukka was still in dragon form. He'd expected her to be at Drekhelm by now.

But even as he was thinking that, an image suddenly came into focus, and he was looking at the Great Hall at Drekhelm—scene of more than one showdown with the Dragonmeet, and of the battle between his classmates and the dragons. She must have just landed and transformed.

She turned, and he saw Mikkel and Theo land behind her, one at a time, shifting quickly into boys.

Bryn, Isabina, and Ferdie had remained back at Cloudhaven, in case everything went wrong today, so those humans left behind would have a chance to get away somewhere safe.

Of course, if the dragons, wolves, and humans went to war, who knew if anywhere would be safe?

Meanwhile, at Drekhelm, the Dragonmeet was assembled around its long table at the other end of the room, its members mid-conversation. Voices were raised, and several of them were standing, as if they were readying themselves to leave. But everyone fell silent as they realized who the three new arrivals were.

Valerius was the first to respond. He was a big, blond man, his hair pulled back into two braids, just like Ellukka's. He rose to his feet and vaulted the table, cradling his still-injured arm against him as he ran toward his daughter.

For several moments, the only view Anders had through the communicator was the front of Valerius's tunic as he hugged Ellukka against him, holding her tight.

"You are in *so* much trouble," he said quietly, "that I don't even know how to describe it. But I'm so happy you're safe."

Then Torsten's voice sounded from behind him. "What have you three been up to?" he demanded. "We were expecting to see you days ago. You're just in time to join us in the attack. I'm sure you'll want to prove your loyalty."

Valerius released his daughter, and Anders could see the Dragonmeet once more. Very few of them looked anything less than threatening.

When Ellukka spoke, her voice was humble. "We've been up to . . . we've done things we shouldn't have," she said quietly.

Mikkel joined in beside her. "We were wrong, we

know that now. We'll accept whatever punishment you give us. We *do* want to show you we're loyal."

"Let's not be hasty," said Leif, coming to his feet, concern all over his face.

Mylestom rose as well, and beside him, Anders could see Saphira's horrified expression. All three of them must be afraid that Ellukka, Mikkel, and Theo really had broken, had decided to come back to Drekhelm and seek forgiveness, abandoning their wolf allies. Perhaps Leif thought he'd made a mistake in telling the children that the Dragonmeet was threatening to attack—that knowing they'd run out of time, they were panicking.

It wasn't such an impossible thing, after all. Living at Cloudhaven, away from their friends and family and everything they knew, had been hard. Others might have given up.

"Why have you come back now?" Torsten asked. "Why today?"

It was Theo's turn to answer. "Because we have information you need to know, and it's urgent," he said.

Leif tried again. "Are you sure—"

"What information?" Valerius demanded. Anders could tell from the angle he was on that he still had an arm around Ellukka.

"We know exactly where Anders and Rayna and Lisabet are going to be soon," she said. "We'll show you, but we don't have much time."

"And it's a small place," Mikkel added, "only a few of you will fit."

"Then we should act quickly," Valerius said. "The Dragonmeet will need to empower a small group of us to act."

"I will be part of it," said Leif firmly. "I am the Drekleid. I am the leader of the Dragonmeet."

A woman from farther along the table spoke up. "Let's make a list of the aspects of this issue that we should discuss," she suggested.

"There's no *time* for that," Theo insisted.

For once, Torsten was on their side. "No time at all," he agreed. "The traitors must be captured."

"I will be going with Leif," said Valerius. "It was my daughter who brought us the news."

Leif nodded. "I propose we bring Torsten and Saphira as well. Then both ends of the debate will be represented, and the decisions that are made will be fair."

Anders knew exactly why Leif was proposing this. Torsten would cheerfully have incinerated the lot of them, given the chance. Saphira felt exactly the opposite—Leif must be hoping that he and Saphira could protect the children.

"We have to hurry," insisted Ellukka, cutting off further discussion.

Leif nodded, coming out from behind the table. "Then let's go," he said simply.

Anders caught a glimpse of Torsten rising to join him, and Saphira wheeling toward the ramp at the end of the table. Then Ellukka's communicator went blank once more, as she shifted to dragon form.

Next, Anders spoke Sakarias's name quietly into the communicator.

The view from the front of his friend's cloak was of the wolves' camp, which he was walking toward. He couldn't see the others, but he knew Viktoria would be beside him, with Det, Mateo, and Jai close behind. The five wolves had insisted on sticking together to do this, more comfortable as a small pack, even if they were exiled from the larger.

Their plan was very simple. Unlike the dragons, they didn't need to do any talking or any convincing. They only needed to be seen by the guards, and then run for the meeting spot—the wolves were guaranteed to chase them.

After all, Anders and Lisabet had betrayed the pack by

stealing Fylkir's chalice and defending the dragons when Ennar had led the class against them. The rest of his friends had betrayed the pack by defending Anders and the others against Sigrid at the Battle of Holbard. All of them were wanted now, so all they had to do was run.

Oh. And not be caught along the way.

The guards would follow, and Anders was sure that Ennar and the others would join in the chase. Anders was hoping that Ennar would try to make sure the children weren't hurt. They had all been her students, after all, and not so long ago.

As Sakarias drew nearer to the camp, Anders saw it had been set up with absolute precision. There were no tents—they were not needed, as the wolves could sleep under the stars in wolf form and be perfectly comfortable.

Anders did wonder where the human staff from Ulfar Academy and Ulfar barracks were, though. Wouldn't they need tents? Perhaps they had been left, or sent, to join the town camp. That was the problem with wolves. They only thought about the pack.

There had been small shelters erected to safeguard the wolves' supplies, but there was very little to block anyone's line of sight.

"Anders," Sakarias muttered, "if you're watching, I really hope this works."

A moment later, they were spotted by the guards, and the howl went up.

"Stop. Traitors!"

Sakarias whirled around and away from them, and Anders could see the others already in wolf form and starting to run. His communicator went blank as he transformed as well.

Now there was nothing to do but hope.

Rayna nudged her brother as a shape appeared on the horizon. It was Hayn—big, even as a wolf—and as he reached them, he slowed to a trot and then slid into human form.

"How's the plan going?" he asked.

"The wolves and dragons are on their way," Anders replied. "Now we just have to hope Sak and the others can stay ahead of the wolves, and that Jerro and Sam can pull off their part."

This was, in some ways, the riskiest piece of the plan. The wolves and dragons could at least guarantee that they'd be able to speak to their leaders, even though that didn't mean they'd be able to convince them. Before Jerro and Sam could do anything, they had to find a way to even get near the mayor, and that was far from guaranteed.

But since the first day they'd rescued Sam and Pellarin,

Anders had known that they couldn't just ignore the humans. The wolves and dragons had done that for far too long. Now, they had to include them. Everyone had to have a voice.

He spoke Sam's name into his communicator, and after a moment, he came into view. Or, rather, Jerro did, as seen from the front of Sam's shirt.

Jerro was holding a knife, which was unexpected, and cutting a hole in what looked like thick, expensive fabric. After a moment, Anders realized it was the back of the mayor's tent.

"Are we sure this is a good idea?" Sam whispered.

Jerro looked back over his shoulder. "Have you got a better one? They're counting on us."

"I can't believe we're trying one of Rayna's ideas," Sam muttered. "I mean, we're talking about the girl famous for running barrel races through the fish market. Maybe we should try the assistants out by the front again."

"They told us to go to the back of the queue," his big brother pointed out. "Unless the others can somehow entertain the wolves and the dragons for two or three days, that won't work. And you have to admit, the barrel races worked. We ate better than the mayor that night."

He pulled aside the fabric and startled as he discovered

a woman waiting on the other side to greet them. "Can I help you?" she said coldly.

"We're here to see the mayor," Sam said, sounding almost confident.

"This isn't the door," she informed them.

"It's *a* door," Jerro replied. "Well, it's a door now, anyway."

"Go to the front of the tent," she said firmly. "You can join the line there."

"It's urgent," Sam insisted, stepping up beside his brother. "We can't wait, or we never would have done this, we promise."

"Everyone's problem is urgent," she replied with a sigh.

Then a voice came from behind her. "Just a moment, Lovisa." The mayor came into sight, looking the same as he had the day Anders had met him, but perhaps a little more tired. "It might actually be urgent," he continued. "They did just cut a hole in our tent, after all."

"You want to hear this," Jerro promised. "Do you want to know where the wolves and dragons who destroyed Holbard are? Because we know where they are right now. Together. But they won't be for long."

The mayor straightened. "This is our chance," he said.

"Are you joking?" Lovisa demanded. "They'll kill us."

The mayor shook his head. "That's a risk I'm willing to take. They *have* to hear our voices," he said. "I won't let us be caught in the middle of their fighting one more day. I've recently learned to listen to my people, and now the wolves and the dragons are going to learn to listen too."

"Then, Herro Mayor," said Sam, "we really have to hurry."

CHAPTER FIFTEEN

ANDERS PACED AND CHECKED THE WRAPPINGS on the Mirror of Hekla again. And when he looked up, he realized he could see the dragons on the horizon.

Lisabet came up to stand beside him. "You can do this," she murmured.

"I'm scared," he admitted quietly.

"That's okay," she replied. "It's scary."

"Are you all right?" He glanced across at her—her eyes were still red, her face white.

"Not really," she said. "But I will be. We both will be. You can do this, Anders." She lifted her chin, as if she were saying something daring. "Your mother isn't the only one who's proud of you."

She turned and walked back to where Rayna and Hayn were sitting together by the boulders, and when she sank down beside them, Hayn wrapped an arm around each of the girls.

Anders walked out to the middle of the circle to stand by the mirror and waited.

Out of everyone, he was the one who had betrayed the wolves *and* the dragons. He had to be the bait they saw, the one who would convince them to enter the circle.

Once they entered the circle, of course, they wouldn't see anyone but themselves.

After a little while of watching the dragons arrow in toward them from above, Anders began to make out the smaller shapes of his friends out in front, and then Rayna called to him from her place by the rocks. "Over there! I can see the wolves!"

Their friends were racing toward them, visibly exhausted by the effort of staying ahead of the Wolf Guard. They were just managing it, though Ennar and a dozen of the Wolf Guard were in hot pursuit and not far behind them now.

The younger wolves went hurtling toward the rocks at the edge of the circle, then around behind the big pile of boulders where Rayna, Hayn, and Lisabet sat. Anders knew his friends must have turned to humans as soon as they crossed the line that Rayna had traced out with the

Staff of Reya—but they made sure that Ennar and the Wolf Guard didn't see it happen.

Ennar and the others pulled up some distance away, and while her followers growled low in their throats, Ennar slipped into human form. "Hayn," she called, ignoring Anders, though she certainly had one eye on him, "what is this?"

Hayn's voice was loud enough to carry, but calm. "This is me asking you to just wait a minute," he replied. "It isn't what you think."

Beside Ennar, one of the Wolf Guard, a man Anders didn't know, transformed as well. He jabbed a finger in Hayn's direction. "He betrayed the Fyrstulf," he shouted, looking at Ennar as though he couldn't believe she wasn't attacking already. "He delayed the search for augmenters. He deliberately slowed her down. That's why she imprisoned him."

Hayn didn't raise his voice, but stayed calm. "We've been friends a very long time, Ennar," he said.

"And that's why I haven't attacked yet," she said, finally looking across at Anders.

"Professor Ennar," he said, "we never meant for any of this to happen. You told us, when we were training at Ulfar, and when you attacked Drekhelm, that you would do anything to protect your students."

"I think," said Ennar slowly, "you are badly misunderstanding what I want to protect them *from*."

But neither she nor Anders got any further. The wolf beside her broke in again, and this time when he shouted, he was pointing at the sky. "Dragons," he cried. "Dragons overhead."

By now, the dragons were circling in to land, touching down one after another, not far away. They stayed in draconic form—all the easier to breathe fire if they needed to—and began to move forward, drawing snarls, snaps, and growls from the wolves.

"Wait," said Ennar warily, holding up one hand, though it wasn't clear whether she was speaking to the wolves or the dragons.

Valerius, Torsten, Leif, and Saphira were out in front, and as each of them crossed the line into the circle, they suddenly, involuntarily, turned to humans. Behind them, Ellukka, Mikkel, and Theo slipped into their human forms, and walked across to join Hayn, Lisabet, and Rayna.

"What's this?" Torsten demanded, looking down at himself in shock, as beside him, Leif politely offered Saphira her chair and helped her into it.

"This is treachery," snapped Valerius. "This is betrayal."

The wolves began to run forward, and as each of

them crossed the invisible line, those who weren't already human also transformed, suddenly finding themselves on two legs, stumbling to catch their balance.

"I can't change back," Valerius cried, staring down at himself.

"What have you done?" Torsten demanded.

"Ah," said Leif calmly.

"I see," said Saphira. "How fascinating. I wonder how far up it goes? You wouldn't want to change in midair without expecting it."

"Gosh," murmured Anders, "I hadn't thought of that."

"Was the artifact your mother's?" Leif asked him. "There's probably a safety mechanism in there somewhere."

He got no further with that conversation, though. Ennar rounded on him with none of the patience she had for Hayn, baring her teeth. "I don't know what your plan is," she said, "but it won't work. You dragons can kill all of us. The rest of our pack will still fight."

"This betrayal was yours," Torsten threw back at her, "and if we don't return, the rest of the Dragonmeet will avenge us."

"Nobody has to avenge anybody," Anders insisted. "That's what we're trying to—"

"Well," said another voice, "this looks cozy."

As they turned around one by one, they saw the mayor and a group of his aides all approaching, their expressions grim.

Valerius dismissed them with a wave of his hand. "Humans," he said, as though the very word meant that they were not worth any more attention.

"This is the *leader* of the humans," Ennar corrected him, "from Holbard. Herro Mayor, leave this to us."

Slowly, the mayor shook his head. "Ennar, I don't think I will. Your pack has made enough decisions on our behalf, and now we have no homes. I'm sick of being afraid, and I'm sick of being silent."

Anders tried again. "I—" But he was completely drowned out by the argument rising all around him. "I—"

He could see his friends watching from behind the rocks, but he couldn't get a word in edgewise as voices rose and threats flew.

He was letting them down. They had brought everyone here, and he wasn't playing his part.

He locked eyes with Rayna, and she pointed to the Mirror of Hekla, still carefully wrapped. *You can do this,* her eyes said.

Anders dropped to one knee and pulled aside the wrapper, baring the mirror to the sky.

Everyone around him fell silent with a gasp, staring

around the circle, eyes wide.

All Anders could see was a few dozen versions of himself, each of them wearing almost identical expressions of confusion and concern.

The one he knew was Valerius had his mouth open. The one he knew was Torsten—who must be seeing dozens upon dozens of Torstens—stepped up to Ennar and gently poked one finger at the air beneath her chin. But despite what his eyes told him, his touch must have confirmed there was no beard there. Ennar bared her teeth, and Anders saw a version of himself growling like a wolf.

Everyone was confused, but for a moment, nobody was speaking.

This was his chance.

He raised his voice. "I'm the one you came here to find," he said, "but I'm not the one who brought you here. You were brought here by wolves and dragons and humans, all working together. Wolves and dragons and humans who have learned to be friends. To respect one another and to protect one another, even though we're different.

"At first, we thought those differences would keep us apart, and that they *should* keep us apart. That the others weren't like us, and it was better to live separately. We were scared of one another. But now we know those differences are what make us so strong that we—just a group of children—have managed to get the leaders of the wolves, dragons, and humans in the same place for the first time since the last great battle. We learned that our ideas are stronger and better if we argue about them, if we forge them in the fire of debate, and share our different points of view so we can find the best way to do something.

"It took us wolves and dragons a while to learn to trust one another, but in time, we did. Then we realized we'd been leaving the humans out of it, thinking we should make decisions *for* them, instead of *with* them.

"The past ten years might have been a fight between ice wolves and scorch dragons, but this whole thing started because the wolves wanted to control the humans—or at least, they didn't think the humans could take care of themselves, and nobody has ever thought so since. Nobody's tried to talk to the humans, but we have to. *Human* isn't an insult. We're all humans, but the ones who aren't elementals have to be smart and tough.

"The wolves and dragons and humans who are my friends learned that groups are fairer and stronger if they're made up of different types of people, who have different ideas about how things should be.

"My sister and I, we're half wolf and half dragon. Our father was Felix. Our mother was Drifa."

A gasp went around the circle, and Rayna rose to her feet, walking across to stand beside him, her chin up, as if she were defying anyone to interrupt him. He didn't give them the chance—he kept talking.

"The fact that Rayna and I are wolf and dragon—and we grew up among humans—means we come from the place where all those things meet. We come from the differences, and the disagreements, and from the strongest part of every point of view. We've come from the place where those things clash. We're battle born, and we're proud of it.

"The group that brought you here is battle born, and so are our goals. We all have different points of view. We all grew up in different ways. And we're smarter together because of those differences. We can do things together— find artifacts, even *create* artifacts, protect people, imagine a different way to live—because we're battle born. It makes us strong.

"At first, we thought that things would be all right if we could only keep you all apart. If we could use the Sun Scepter to balance out the Snowstone, so nobody would have the advantage, and everybody would just continue the way they were, separate.

"But we were wrong, and not just because of what happened to Holbard when we tried that. The answer was never to keep wolves and dragons and humans apart. What we need is for everyone to come *together*. We need all of you to talk to one another, to listen, to see past all the lies, and realize"—he gestured around, knowing that everyone could only see themselves—"that there's a part of you in everyone here."

He turned his gaze to where Hayn stood, and his uncle nodded silent encouragement. "Our parents worked together," Anders continued, "to create and restore the artifacts we're using today. And just yesterday, wolves and dragons worked on them again. It was so *we* could come together and forge something new.

"The new Vallen can be battle born. The dragons take so long to decide anything that nothing ever happens. The wolves follow their pack leader without question. And sometimes that pack leader makes mistakes, and there's nobody to say so. The humans don't trust either of them, but they also don't try to talk to them—and even if they did, nobody would listen.

"We've all lived in those worlds, and our friends come from all of them. And you have a *lot* to learn from each other. Wolves and dragons are meant to work together to create artifacts. Designers and dragonsmiths are no good without each other. And the humans are the families wolves and dragons come from.

"Dragons know that differences are important—it's why every student at their school studies something different, why the Dragonmeet talks and talks until every voice is heard. And wolves and humans know too—they live in Holbard, where there are people from all over the world, making the city stronger and more interesting with the things and ideas they bring from other countries.

"Right now, you're all separate. Most of you don't have anywhere to live, and you're all spending a lot of time worrying about being attacked. So maybe, just *maybe*, you should all stop looking for someone to blame, and start talking instead.

"If you don't agree, then argue! Forge a new way to do this with a battle of *words*. The new Vallen *has* to be battle born, and it will be a better place to live for all of us."

Everyone was completely silent when Anders stopped speaking. He had never said so many words in a row in his entire life.

Beside him, Rayna was holding his hand so tight, he thought she'd break his fingers. But he knew what it meant. *I'm so proud of you, I can't even talk, so I have to try to break your hand to show you.*

He half hoped that Leif would say something, or Hayn, but he knew why they didn't. They were already the most inclined to listen to him, but they couldn't drag everyone else along with them. They weren't the ones he had to convince.

So he held his breath as Torsten and Valerius, now just two versions of himself, looked at each other, as Ennar eyed the mayor, who stared straight back.

And then Valerius looked at the version of himself who was really Ellukka, and he seemed to decide something. "Well," he said, "I can't do this while I'm staring at a dozen versions of my own face. I'm just not that good looking. And I can only imagine what it's like for Torsten, staring at that many versions of his beard."

The version of Anders that was Torsten actually snorted, amused. But when he spoke, he sounded stern. "We're not just going to give things away. We're the ones who have somewhere to live. We're not the ones coming asking for help."

"Nobody's asking for help," Ennar replied quickly.

"Once upon a time," said Saphira mildly, "they wouldn't have *had* to ask for help."

Anders stayed silent, watching. Every single one of them was hearing what everyone else said, as though it came from their own lips. Saphira's reminder had been spoken to each of them in their own voice.

It wasn't that they'd forgotten who the others were, or that they really thought they were speaking to themselves.

But perhaps seeing themselves speak, instead of someone they had always automatically assumed was wrong, it was just a little bit harder to completely dismiss it. Perhaps, hearing the words come from their own lips, they were forced to consider them just a little bit more carefully.

"You know what?" said the mayor, folding his arms. "I'll ask for help. I'm not too proud. My people don't have anywhere to live anymore. Two groups of elementals destroyed our city, and I don't care if they were trying to hurt us or trying to protect us. What I care about is that we're hungry, and my duty is to provide for my people any way I can."

"We have a duty too," said Ennar. "To protect you."

"This isn't about your duty," said the mayor firmly. "This is about the fact that we're all Vallenites."

Anders looked across at Hayn, who slowly lifted a finger to his lips. *Stay silent*, his face—or, rather, Anders's face—said. *Let them keep talking.*

Behind Hayn, two more versions of Anders that he was pretty sure were Sam and Sakarias were energetically jumping up and down in celebration. Anders wasn't sure it was time for that yet, but at least nobody was attacking anybody else.

Tentatively, he crouched down and began to wrap the mirror back up again. It had done its job. It had reminded them that, in some ways, they were all the same.

Now it was time for them to see their differences again. To talk and debate. And, in battles of words and ideas, to work out what kind of Vallen they wanted to live in. Now they had to show each other their differences, because *those* were where the best ideas would come from.

All the adults paused as Anders finished wrapping up the mirror, suddenly seeing one another clearly again.

And then, as he picked it up and quietly backed away toward his friends . . .

. . . they all kept talking.

EPILOGUE

Five months later

ANDERS SAT ON A HILL ABOVE HOLBARD, SIDE BY side with Lisabet, eating slices of Kaleb's cake. They were near the place that Sigrid had been buried, overlooking the city.

In the end, he and Rayna had decided not to tell anyone what Sigrid had done. They couldn't hurt Sigrid now. She was gone. But telling the world *would* hurt Lisabet. And it wouldn't bring back Felix or Drifa.

Their mother's ashes had been scattered high above Vallen, to travel the winds as she had loved to do. But he and Rayna still had the portrait from her workshop, hers and Felix's augmenters, and a growing collection of other things the dragons had been unearthing and gifting to Drifa's children.

And, just as importantly, he and Rayna had Hayn.

So, too, did Lisabet; and Sam, Jerro, and Pellarin; and many of the other children who had sheltered at Cloudhaven.

"I've missed having a family," Hayn had said the other day, looking around at all of them ruefully. "I wished I could have one again. I just didn't imagine it would come true on quite this scale."

Still, he never seemed to mind for a moment.

Ennar took a close interest in Anders, Rayna, and Lisabet as well—though she was no longer Professor Ennar. After the new trials, she had become the Fyrstulf, and the leader of the wolves.

She and Leif and the mayor were mostly getting along well. She and the mayor thought Leif was far too relaxed. Leif and the mayor thought Ennar was far too intense. Ennar and Leif still occasionally forgot to ask the mayor's opinion, but he quickly reminded them when that happened.

Ennar's wife kept cooking everyone dinner and feeding them during negotiations, and, as Sakarias said, "It's hard to disagree when your mouth's full of dessert."

"You'd know," Viktoria had replied dryly.

But today was special, and Anders wasn't thinking about any of that. Yesterday, a ship carrying a troupe of stone bears from Allemhäut had arrived. In their human form they'd looked like an ordinary assortment of people, mostly clad in the brightly colored clothes of their homeland, all reds and blues and greens, small flowers embroidered along their hems.

In their elemental form they were huge, shaggy brown bears with dark eyes and enormous paws. Today the bears had set to work mending the cracks in the ground that divided Holbard into sections, rising onto their back legs and lifting their front paws, moving the rock and stone as easily as the wolves sent an ice spear flying through the air.

It had been a rough voyage from Allemhäut, and a rough entry into the harbor, but soon that would change. A team of designers and dragonsmiths, led by Hayn, Tilda, and a still-grumpy Kaleb, was working on repairing the wind arches that had protected the harbor until recently. Huge sweeps of metal, painstakingly forged and engraved with runes, stretched from one side of the harbor mouth to the other, and soon they would once again ensure that the waters inside were always calm. It was that guaranteed calm harbor in Holbard that had made the city such a mix of people from all over the world—merchant ships came from everywhere, knowing they could safely dock when they arrived.

Anders could pick out Rayna and Ellukka among the

dragons wheeling above the city, playing and watching the stone bears' progress. He knew their other friends would have found perches and places to watch as well.

But some of them would be at the other great construction site, inside the city walls, in the place where the old Ulfar Academy had once been.

Long ago, Lisabet had pointed out that the Ulfar courtyard had been built large enough for a dragon to land. Proof, she had said, that the wolves had once welcomed the dragons. Now, that courtyard would be even larger. The site would be home to the Vallenskól, where wolves, dragons, and humans would study side by side. A second campus was already under construction up in the mountains, at Old Drekhelm, a place for the students to travel in summer, or when their lessons required a little more altitude or space.

Anders and his friends would be among the first pupils of the school. He was one part nervous, one part excited, and one part disbelieving that this was somehow happening.

But before their classes began, they had a break to celebrate the equinox.

It was hard to believe that last equinox he had been desperately making his way toward Drekhelm to rescue Rayna, terrified she was about to be sacrificed by the very dragons who were now his friends.

"This equinox," Rayna had said, "we're going to party like dragons, reflect like wolves, and eat like humans."

"I think we have to," Mikkel had agreed solemnly.

"It's our duty to embrace the best of all worlds," Sam agreed.

With a rumble down below, a huge crack in the ground heaved, shifted, and closed, sealing up as though it had never been there.

"That was amazing," Lisabet breathed. "Let's go and watch up close."

"All right," Anders agreed, popping his last bite of Kaleb's cake into his mouth.

Lisabet shifted to wolf form and began trotting down the hill.

Anders watched her go for a moment. Of all the wonderful things that had happened in the last year, his best friend—smart and loyal and strong—might just be the most wonderful of all, he thought.

Stones shifted again down below him in the city, and with the sound of Holbard's repairs ringing in his ears, he grinned and transformed, then chased her down the hill.

ACKNOWLEDGMENTS

I wish we could stay in the world of Vallen forever—I hope you've enjoyed your time there as much as I have!

No story is ever told by the author alone, and I'll take this last chance to thank the people who helped introduce you to Anders and his friends.

My editor, Andrew Eliopulos, was—as ever—endlessly imaginative, patient, and supportive, and I find such joy in working with him. Abby Ranger began this journey with me, and her touch is still to be found in every part of it.

The crew at Harper have taken such wonderful care of me—from sales and marketing to production to art, thank you all! In particular, thank you to Rosemary Brosnan; Bria Ragin; Joe Merkel and Levente Szabo for my gorgeous cover design and artwork; Virginia Allyn for a map that ended up shaping this story; and Jill Amack and Caitlin Lonning for saving me from my many mistakes. Thank you to the fantastic crew at Harper Oz, who have been such wonderful pack members along the way.

My pack at Adams Literary is a part of everything I do—Tracey, Josh, Cathy, and Stephen, thank you!

To the readers, reviewers, booksellers, and librarians who share my stories with others—thank you, thank you, thank you. I see and appreciate everything you do!

This book was written while I was pregnant, a situation that presented some new challenges on top of the usual ones. Without my friend Liz Barr, it couldn't have been done—when I couldn't type, she made sense of my dictation! Thank you, Liz.

Meg Spooner's stamp is on everything I do, and on this book more than most I owe her a debt of gratitude for a wonderful brainstorming session that helped me find just the key I needed to begin. Here's to many more days at hot springs around the world!

Will and Ned Marney lent me their thoughts as well as their middle names for this series—I hope you like the finale!

Thank you as well to the other friends who lent me the support I needed to do justice to the end of this story I love so much—Jay, Marie, Leigh, Michelle, Kacey, Nic, Cat, Soraya, Ryan, Peta, Eliza, Kate A., the Roti Boti gang, the House of Progress crew, and of course Kate I., to whom this book is dedicated. I'm incredibly grateful to have such a list of friends. For this series in particular, the list wouldn't be complete without my team of incredibly talented mediators at FOS, who taught me each day how to see things from a different point of view.

My family has always been unwavering in their support, and this book has been no exception—I'm so lucky to have you.

And finally, Brendan and Pip! As I write these acknowledgments I can hear you playing together, practicing sounds that are coming very close to the one I'm most excited to hear: Ma-ma-ma! I love you both more than I knew was possible. I can't wait for all the adventures we'll have together.

Read the full Elementals series by
AMIE KAUFMAN

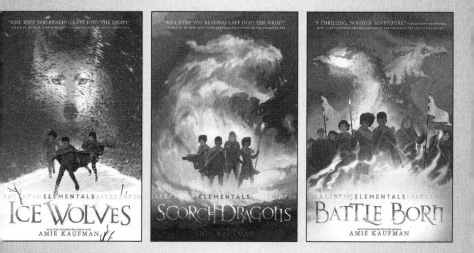